The Lion
of Modderspruit

The Lion
of Modderspruit

by Lawrence Penning

INHERITANCE PUBLICATIONS
NEERLANDIA, ALBERTA, CANADA
PELLA, IOWA, U.S.A.

National Library of Canada Cataloguing in Publication

Penning, L. (Louwrens), 1854-1927.
 The Lion of Modderspruit / by Lawrence Penning ; [translated
by Marietjie Nelson].

 (The Louis Wessels commando ; #1)
 Translation of: Leeuw van Modderspruit.
 ISBN 1-894666-91-7

 1. South African War, 1899-1902—Juvenile fiction.
I. Nelson, Marietjie II. Title. III. Series.
PZ7.P39Li 2004   j839.3'1362   C2004-901703-9

Library of Congress Cataloging-in-Publication Data

Penning, L. (Louwrens), 1854-1927
 [Leeuw van Modderspruit. English.]
 The Lion of Modderspruit / by Lawrence Penning ; [translated by
Marietjie Nelson].
    p. cm. — (The Louis Wessels commando ; #1)
 Summary: As the second Boer War intensifies in 1899, twenty-three-year-
old Afrikaner, Louis Wessels, becomes known as the Lion of Modderspruit
for his heroic conduct during this crucial victory for the Boers.
    ISBN 1-894666-91-7 (pbk.)
    1. South African War, 1899-1902—Juvenile fiction. [1. South African
War, 1899-1902—Fiction. 2. South Africa—History—1836-1909—Fiction.
3. Afrikaners—Fiction. 4. War—Fiction. 5. Christian life—Fiction.] I.
Nelson, Marietjie. II. Title.
PZ7.P38513Li 2004
[Fic]—dc22

                                                            2004002135

Originally published as De leeuw van Modderspruit

Translated by Marietjie Nelson
Cover Painting *Transvaal Boer leaving his family for the war* by Lydia J.
Kruidhof

Published simultaneously in U.S.A. by Inheritance Publications
Box 366, Pella, Iowa 50219

Available in Australia from Inheritance Publications
Box 1122, Kelmscott, W.A. 6111 Tel. & Fax (089) 390 4940

Printed in Canada

Contents

Glossary of Afrikaans Words

Afrikaner: Afrikaans-speaking white person in South Africa

Biltong: meat that is salted and cut into strips and dried; jerky

Blikoor: Nickname for someone living in the Orange Free State.

Boer: Farmer — a South African of Dutch or Huguenot descent, especially one of the early settlers of the Transvaal and the Orange Free State

Kraal: enclosure for the protection of livestock.

Polder: a piece of land reclaimed from the sea or a river

Redneck: Nickname for an English person

Redcoat: Nickname for an English soldier (who wore red coats in the first Anglo Boer War)

Sjambok: whip

Transvaaler: Boer living in the Transvaal

Uitlander: foreign immigrant living in the Transvaal

Veld: open country, field

Voortrekkers: Pioneers, or Leading Migrants; the Afrikaners who left the British Cape Colony in southern Africa to make the Great Trek into the interior

Chapter I
Threatening Skies

It was afternoon. The sun was burning down from the sky, piercing the countryside with its sharp light. Not a cloud was in sight. Above the hard, dry, undulating fields stood a glaring sky. The tufts of long spiky tembu grass waved sluggishly to and fro. Both riders were very hot as they cantered over the wide, lonely dirt road. Their small horses, which had already made a long trip, allowed their weary heads to hang.

They differed considerably in age, these two horsemen, the elder being at least sixty and the younger not more than thirteen years old. One look was enough to establish that they were closely related. No wonder, since they were father and son.

The village now lay behind them, a small, quiet rural town with uninteresting straight streets, a whitewashed church, low houses, and tarred fences surrounding the *kraal*. The slim little tower could be seen clearly, lifting its pinnacle above the roofs and trees like a finger pointing upward.

The village was built on the hillsides and the road meandered up along them, snaking away to the invisible horizon. At the top of the hills, banks of blazing hot stone reflected the harsh sun.

The elder of the two horsemen was a heavy, muscular man. He had a long beard with a lot of gray in it, and on his stocky head he wore a broad-brimmed hat. His feet were in the stirrups, and the reins lay slack in his right hand. His sharp face was sad and serious while his gray eyes stared ahead sternly.

This was the way Gijs Wessels was known to outsiders: solemn, immovable, and stern. But his friends knew the warm heart beating under the rough exterior. There was no one who looked after his family better than he, and no father was more closely attached to his children.

Young Daniel looked at his father out of the corner of his eye. "I'm thirsty!" he complained.

"Just be patient a little longer," his father said, trying to cheer him up; "we'll reach the creek and the waterfall soon."

So they proceeded in silence, riding side by side, until they came to a place where the murmur of the water became audible.

They soon reached the creek, which came rushing over a cliff at least twelve feet high, the sun sparkling in beautiful colours on the falling water.

Daniel jumped down quickly from his horse and drank long, greedy draughts of the lovely cool water. How good it felt!

His father had also alighted and taking both horses by the reins, led them to the water. Then he hobbled them both and allowed them to graze on the grassy bank. He himself sat down in the cool shade of a thorn tree, where Daniel joined him.

From there one had a broad view of the landscape. The undulating hills went on as far as the eye could see — like one immense sea of waves having suddenly turned to stone. This monotonous view was only broken by the occasional tall tree, low bush, or lonely homestead.

The Boer unfastened a linen bag attached to his saddle. From it he took a huge chunk of brown bread, broke it in half and gave Daniel one piece. The boy tucked in with his strong young teeth, and ate with relish, for he was hungry. No wonder, since for some eight hours he had not had anything, and the Transvaal mountain air gave one an appetite.

Footsteps were approaching. A man was coming along the footpath, a black man, walking on bare feet with a slow dreamlike pace. He was clothed in an old sack in which three holes had been cut — one for his head and two for his arms. The sun burned down on his kinky black hair, angular face, and bare muscular arms, gleaming with the fat with which they had been rubbed.

The path brought him right past the two Transvaalers, and as he reached them, he stretched out his hands, begging for a piece of bread.

It seemed as though Gijs Wessels had not even noticed the black man. Immersed in his own thoughts, he had been staring in a different direction. He had hardly touched his own bread; most of it lay in the bag on the ground, and a swarm of ants were scurrying around over the bag, intent on getting their share. The Boer looked up somewhat surprised on seeing the black man standing before him.

"Master, a piece of bread, please, a piece of bread!"

Wessels pointed in silence to the bag, and the black man greedily took the bread. He thanked them in his own peculiar way, stilled his hunger with the wholesome bread, and then slaked his thirst by scooping up water from the creek in his cupped hands. Refreshed, he went on with lighter steps.

"A Zulu — a strong, hardy people!" said Gijs Wessels to his son, but said nothing else. He took up his pondering attitude again.

What was the Boer thinking of so seriously?

He had been on a visit to his brother-in-law, where he had heard disturbing news on the course the *Uitlander* question was threatening to take. The question arose from a petition signed by twenty-one thousand *uitlanders*, foreign immigrants living in the Transvaal, requesting the intervention of Her Majesty the Queen of Britain, since they were oppressed by the Boers. Yes, "oppressed" was what they called it.

Gijs Wessels pursed his lips, but his face seemed to relax somewhat and a slight, contemptuous smile curved his mouth.

"Twenty-one thousand *uitlanders*," he mumbled to himself, "where would they get that many? Women and children, bastards and blacks, even the deceased must have joined in signing."

His thoughts turned to the gold mines of the Witwatersrand.

"We should have left the gold to rest in the dark bowels of the earth," he mused. "My father was a wise and experienced man. He always warned against mining. He feared that the pounding of machinery would wake up the evil spirits. 'Better poor and free, than rich and enslaved' was his motto, and he was right. Neither does the gold do our nation any good . . ."

The harsh expression disappeared from Wessels' face and in the stern eyes great sorrow was to be seen.

He saw the young Transvaal lapsing from the solid foundation on which the old *Voortrekkers* had stood, and it caused him great sadness.

It was true that religion was still upheld, the churches were attended, the ministers were honoured. Yet with many Boers the soul of the matter was missing. Amid much of the religion, true religion had become something rare.

A dark shadow clouded his broad brow, he clasped his hands together — was he praying for his sinking people?

Then he got up and walked to the top of the hill, looking around for his horses. They were grazing peacefully.

He sat down again in his former place, in the shade of the thorn-tree. He thought once more about the twenty-one thousand *uitlanders* — anger and indignation showed on his sun-browned face.

The *uitlanders* were really nothing but foreigners and strangers who had come to dine at the hospitable table of the Boer, and out of gratitude for the hospitality they now wanted to put the host in shackles. Hadn't many of the complaining *uitlanders* come to Johannesburg like driftwood washing onto the shore, and afterward became millionaires? They complained that they were being oppressed, but while these gold kings were slandering their legal government in their grand villas, most of the Boers remained poor, satisfied with their simple unpretentious houses on the wide lonesome *veld*.

The *uitlanders* were demanding a more extensive franchise. Naturally! So that they could outvote the Boers, take over the government, and drive the Boers into a corner.

"Well, we haven't reached that stage yet!" he suddenly called out loudly, clenching his huge fists.

He stood cool and calm once again, amazed at himself for having been carried away by his anger.

High above him in the air hovered a bird of prey on widespread wings, and at his feet the hardworking ants were busy. They drew his attention. Since childhood he had liked observing the mysterious machinery of nature, which all worked together. To Gijs Wessels the invisible minds of the ants that were trodden underfoot formed one of the greatest miracles of God's power and wisdom.

So he watched the small, insignificant ants, diligently doing their work. He saw an ant stop near a crumb. It tried hard to drag the crumb along with him, but it was too big. The ant disappeared, and presently returned with a fellow worker. Together they set to it, but in vain. The crumb was still too big for them. Then came more help — two more ants — six — twelve — and together they towed away the crumb.

Gijs Wessels kept watching the ants. To him they were becoming like giants, and in them he saw the Dutch Afrikaners living in the immense expanse between Table Bay and the Zambezi River. One ant was unable to conquer this bread crumb, and so were two — but twelve succeeded. For unity brings strength. The Transvaal Boer on his own might be unable to conquer the bread of freedom, and together with the Free State would still be too weak. But if they all worked together, if Rhodesia, Bechuana, Natal, and the Cape Colony — especially the Cape Colony — in unison with the people from Transvaal and the Free State, took up the struggle against British tyranny, then, as far as it was humanly predictable, victory would be certain.

Daniel had fallen asleep. The heat and fatigue had made him drowsy; his head had drooped onto his father's shoulder. Only now did Wessels notice this, and carefully took up position with his back to a rock, so as not to disturb the boy in his sleep. With careful attentiveness he waved off the bothersome flies and he eyed his son lovingly, his youngest, his Benjamin.

He loved all his children, loved them dearly, but this son had something peculiar, something special which set him apart from the others. The father had at one time been worried because never did a hard or rude word against his parents cross Daniel's lips. He seemed to be one of the young plants that ripen early to be transplanted by the great Farmer into the orchards of Heaven. His bodily frame was more frail than that of his brothers, who were as strong as oxen.

Gijs Wessels wrapped his left arm protectively around the boy to prevent him from sliding down, and with his handkerchief swept off the ants crawling up his feet.

In this manner he kept watch for awhile. But his eyes grew heavy, and soon they closed. His left arm was still wrapped around his child. So they sat sleeping, father and son, in the cool shade of the thorn-tree.

Across the *veld* came a hunter at full gallop, while a large hunting dog, barking playfully, preceded him with huge bounds.

Suddenly the dog seemed to have discovered something peculiar. It was sniffing along with its nose to the ground, straight ahead.

The young hunter had reached the crest of a small flat-topped hill. He rose in the stirrups, and seeing the two grazing horses, thought he knew what it was.

"Quiet, Pluto!" he called. "Quiet!"

The dog had now approached the waterfall, looking at his master and wagging his tail.

The young hunter quickly dismounted from his horse, and threw the reins loosely over the neck of his beautiful tall bay stallion.

"Stay!" was all he said, and the noble animal did not move.

Near the waterfall, in the shade of the thorn-tree, he discovered the two sleepers, and with difficulty restrained Pluto. He stood looking at the pair with his arms folded across his chest.

There was no doubt that he was closely related to the two people on the ground. The likeness to the youngest was especially striking, but the young hunter looked altogether sturdier, stronger, and more determined. The almost feminine softness on the face of the thirteen-year-old boy was completely absent from his features. His determined mouth was set in an almost reckless expression. His blue eyes looked the world straight in the eye, and his whole person exuded cheerful confidence. The broad-brimmed brown hat was pushed back, and rested carelessly on his wavy blonde hair. A loaded rifle with a shiny barrel hung from his shoulder. He couldn't have been older than twenty-three years, but he was at least six feet tall, muscular like a young lion, and the zest for life which shone in his eyes sent the blood tingling through his veins.

Among his friends and neighbours he was commonly called "the young hunter" because he was a very keen huntsman, and as a sharpshooter none could beat him.

The sleeping pair drew more than his usual attention. True, they were his brother and father, but that needn't have stopped him from waking them. They were still a long way off from home, their farm *Wonderfontein*,[*] and the sun was already in the west.

---

[*] Afrikaans: *Miraculous Fountain*

Yet he couldn't bring himself to do so. The scene before him was so gripping in its artless simplicity, that he did not feel like disturbing it.

But on the spot where the two were sleeping, the shadow was now shifting. The rays of the evening sun slanted at a different angle now and their light was driving the shadow farther off. Gradually the rays were creeping up on the two sleeping people, and as soon as the light would fall on their faces, they would wake up. Carefully the young hunter took a cloth and spread it over both their faces. In this way the sharp sunlight would not wake them.

Maybe he had not done it carefully enough. The old Boer woke up and looked around bewilderedly.

"Oh, Louis," he said, "is that you? This is a fine how-do-you-do! Here we are loafing about and Mother won't know why we are staying out so long. Come, Daniel; wake up, my boy. We must get into the saddle!"

The three Boers were soon mounted and riding along side by side, the hooves of their horses kicking up clouds of dust. The sun was now floating like a huge ball of flame above the horizon while the shadows of the horsemen and their mounts glided like enormous ghosts over the extensive *veld*.

They spoke little. Gijs Wessels was anxious to be home.

"What's the news from the conference in Bloemfontein?" asked the young hunter. "Have you heard anything about Chamberlain? Is it true that he seems quite meek nowadays?"

"I am afraid we are going to have great problems with England," Gijs Wessels said gravely. "The *uitlanders* are complaining that they are being wronged. They are calling for the intervention of Queen Victoria."

"If they get too much say in matters, we will drive them out of the land!" said Louis, patting down the waving mane of his galloping stallion.

But his father gave no reply.

He had lived through three wars: two against the blacks and one against the British, and he knew the meaning of war. His gaze went slowly over the wide extensive *veld*. The last rays of the setting sun glowed red on that *veld*. As far as his eyes could see everything was painted red — red as blood — the hard rocks, the hills, the valleys — all red as blood . . .

Gijs Wessels spurred on his horse, and the horsemen rode faster now, up hills and down hills, to *Wonderfontein*.

A Boer prepared for Battle

Chapter II
A Conversation

They turned into the long lane flanked by slender poplars. The stars were twinkling in the cloudless heavens and the moon shone like molten silver through the green leaves of the huge lime tree in front of the house.

Mother Wessels, the wife of Gijs Wessels, known among her friends as Aunt Sannie, had already opened the upper door several times to see if her husband was coming, and her friendly but worried face relaxed when she saw the three horsemen trotting into the yard, preceded by the hunting dog barking loudly. She went out to meet them and welcome them. They hurried inside while some of the black servants brought the steaming horses to the stables.

They came into a spacious living room. A crackling fire was burning in the hearth and a modern kerosene lamp was hanging from the ceiling. It gave off a bright, cheerful light, forming a great contrast to the canola oil lamp which had been in use up to the previous year. Actually Gijs was not in favour of the change, but feminine perseverance and feminine guile had persuaded him at last to buy a kerosene lamp in town.

This is the way life goes on. Gijs Wessels' father was grateful in his young days for the poor light of a tallow candle to read a chapter from the well-worn family Bible or a devout meditation by Lodensteyn, but the tallow candle was replaced by a wax candle, and the wax candle by canola oil lamps, and the canola oil lamps by kerosene lamps.

And that was the way the world went on!

But Gijs Wessels was well off — so why not make grateful use of the gifts of God?

He inherited extensive fields from his father, old Lukas Wessels, whose huge portrait had a place of honour above the old armchair to the right of the fireplace.

There had been a time when Lukas Wessels owned nothing apart from the lions, tigers, and snakes on the farm of six thousand acres which the government had given him for free as a voluntary immigrant. But his livestock increased steadily. The cattle plague, a true scourge for South Africa, passed by his *kraals*, and as a wise man who understood that land would increase in value, he put himself out to enlarge his estate. So he first bought a piece of land for five heifers; the next time, a piece, the size of a Dutch *polder*, for four oxen. Every time he came home after such a trading and told his thrifty wife, Aunt Suze, about it, she carefully wiped her horn-rimmed spectacles, shook her head inside her large black bonnet and said in a warning tone: "Luke, Luke, we will become paupers through these transactions of yours!"

Yet slowly Aunt Suze was proved quite wrong. Lukas Wessels became a great land-owner, and although what he had bought was wilderness, that wilderness became more valuable as the population increased. That was exactly what old Lukas Wessels had counted on without ever taking into account what an exorbitant price the land would fetch should it prove to contain veins of gold.

For at the time there had been no hint of gold diggings. It is true that the old *Voortrekkers* had often whispered to one another that there had to be rich gold mines in the Transvaal soil, but nobody seemed to know anything in particular about it, and the old Boers left it at that. A vague premonition told them that evil spirits under the earth would wake up if the precious metal which was resting in the bosom of the earth should be brought up into the sunlight above. But when inquisitive *uitlanders* did determine the presence of rich amounts of gold, the mining process could in the end not be held back any longer. Lukas Wessels sold one of his farms in the Witwatersrand for twenty-five thousand pounds sterling. The company who bought the farm called the price monstrously high but refused a new offer of a competing firm who had offered them a profit of a hundred thousand pounds sterling, with the message "We are no fools!"

So Lukas Wessels had suddenly become a rich man. He had sold a barren piece of wilderness for three thousand guilders, and still had seven farms left — one for each child.

Yet the pleasure of this uncommon prosperity did not balance with his rising concern for the fate of his people. Lukas Wessels, whose stern face and tight lips looked out from the faded old portrait above the old armchair, was truly a genuine *Voortrekker*, with his eyes wide open to the terrible danger attached to the possession of gold. For he had already noticed how the sudden excessive prosperity was undermining the true power of the Boer, cutting through the locks of the Afrikaans Samson. On the other hand, it could be foreseen that Ahab's thirst for gold and hunger for land would be stimulated by Naboth's rich vineyard.

Lukas Wessels had passed away three years earlier. He had died in the old armchair next to the hearth where Gijs Wessels was now sitting.

It had been a lovely sunny day, that last day of his life. The battle at Krugersdorp had just been fought. Johannesburg, the Judas, had bent its proud neck and the commandos were coming home, triumphant after the short struggle. One of these commandos was just passing through on the main road which was linked to *Wonderfontein* by the lane. The officer in command was in front with his lieutenants, and behind them were the Boers, rifles on their right hips in closely linked ranks. On his bed the dying old patriarch heard their song in marching tempo:

High up in our clear blue skies
Unfurl the freedom banner of Transvaal!
The enemy has been put to flight
It is a day of shining joy!

Hearing the song the old *Voortrekker* could no longer stay in bed. The waning light of his life flared up once more — for the last time. He was carried to the armchair by his son Gijs, and through the small window-panes he had once more seen the Four Colours of his country fluttering in the midst of the horsemen. Standing on the threshold of eternity, he uttered the prophesy which had been given by God Himself as an indestructible, comforting promise in the heart of the suffering and struggling Afrikaans people: "It is going to be all right! Africa for the Afrikaners!"

Gijs Wessels had now taken off his heavy black riding boots and set them down by the corner of the big square oak table, where he sat facing the cosy fire. Aunt Sannie was sitting next to him, at the table, and was busy refreshing the travellers with hot, good-smelling coffee and lovely cold mutton and bread — tasty brown bread that she had made herself.

Fifteen-year-old Janske sat across from her mother quietly knitting socks. Kees, twenty years old, and Karel, eighteen, were sitting with their brothers Louis and Daniel by the fireplace.

Two more men were sitting by the fireplace, but they were deep in shadow and only when the fire flared up now and again did their faces become clearly visible.

The evening meal had now been finished, and Master Wessels was enquiring about his livestock: about the white calf which had injured a leg the previous week, about his beautiful brown horse which seemed to be getting distemper, and about the amount of wool brought in by his three thousand sheep which his workers were busy shearing. As a careful farmer he enquired about everything on his land, and now that he was done, he filled his wooden pipe and lit it with a long burning splinter.

For a few moments silence reigned. Pluto had stretched himself out on the iron plate right in front of the feet of the young hunter. The chirping sound of crickets behind the fireplace could be heard.

One of the men in the shadow was the first to break the silence.

"How is it nowadays with the Rednecks, Cousin?"

"I foresee that we will have trouble with them, Albert!"

"If they become too cheeky, I foresee that they will have more trouble with *us* than we with *them*."

"You are underestimating the power of England," said Gijs Wessels calmly.

Albert plucked off a dry leaf from a branch he threw on the fire.

"This is what we will do with them!" he said, while crushing the dry leaf in his heavy fist.

The three elder sons burst out laughing loudly. They represented courageous young Transvaal, itching to try its youthful strength against unjust England. But Daniel with his soft sad eyes did not laugh, and neither did old Wessels, because he saw farther than his brave sons.

"You are underestimating the power of England," he repeated gravely. "I was once in the vast city of London and I stood on one of its high towers. There was a sea of houses at my feet, an immense, wide sea of houses. As I stood on this tower the edge of the veil was lifted for me and my heart trembled when I saw the power and riches of England. The city of London alone has more able-bodied men than the whole of our Transvaal people, including men, women and children, and even counting babes in arms."

"You forget about the Free State," said the man in the shadow. "If matters become bad, the Free State will join us."

"Even if you count the Free State," Wessels rejoined, "London alone still numbers more able-bodied men than all of us."

"What kind of men are they!" said the man in the shadow, "Clerks, waiters, and tailors! If they come we will chase them back home with the *sjambok*, the whip."

"It isn't even necessary for England to call up its civilians," said Wessels. "They have a trained army which has fought in all parts of the world."

"Mercenaries, nothing but mercenaries!" said the man in the shadow. "I will personally take on five of those pipsqueaks." And he spat into the fire contemptuously.

"And I will take on six!" Kees added, stretching his strong young muscles.

But old Wessels shook his graying head in warning.

"I don't like this overconfidence," he said. "It's the wrong way to start a war, despising the enemy."

"But don't we have justice on our side? God and justice?" called out the man in the shadow. At that moment the shadow receded, for the fire, which had been newly fed, flared up high, and the black-bearded face and determined expression of the speaker became clearly visible.

"We have God and justice — sacred justice — on our side," he repeated once more. "So whom are we to fear? If war breaks out with England, we will win. As sure as there is a just and almighty God who reigns, we will win."

The passion lurking deep in the heart of the Afrikaans Boer surfaced vehemently, the inner fire in his soul flared up high and in his honest brown eyes the glow of the hearth-fire reflected that inner fire.

But Gijs Wessels was not feeling content.

"Your words are too reckless for me," he said, "although I can understand them."

"And your words are too anxious and hesitating for me," said the man in the shadow, "and that I cannot understand, Uncle Wessels!"

It would have been better to have held back those words.

"How can you talk about anxiety and hesitation?" Wessels answered emphatically, with indignation in his voice. "When you were just a little boy playing at your mother's side, I stormed Amajuba."

The black-bearded man felt his indignation, and regretted his words. He proffered a hand to old Wessels, saying in a conciliatory tone, "I am sorry if I have offended one of the brave men who stormed Amajuba — who ever doubted your boldness?"

Harmony was restored by these generous words.

"But do you doubt that we will win, if it comes to war?" inquired the man in the shadow.

"I'll tell you something," resumed the man of the house, speaking more slowly and guardedly. "Our struggle with England does not date from the present, but from 1815, when the gallows were erected at Slachtersnek for five Afrikaans Boers. The struggle has been going on for more than eighty-four years, and God only knows when the end will come. It is possible that the war which we fear at the moment will form the last link in the long bitter chain, but we cannot look into God's counsel, and we don't know. But that there will finally be a triumph of our rights I do *not* doubt, and I will *never* doubt. Even if the British flag were to fly from the government building in Pretoria, and even if our Republic were overthrown by the violence of England, it would only be temporarily, and the trampled resilience of our nation will bounce back in the Lord's own time, with irresistible force."

He was getting warm while saying this. It was his deepest thoughts he was revealing — it was one of the heroes of Amajuba speaking.

In the deepest shadow, in the opposite corner of the fireplace sat the other man, a stranger.

Nobody knew him. He had been passing with a transport wagon and had asked for hospitality for the night, since he could not bear the jolting of the heavy, creaking ox wagon.

"A feeble chap — a kind of office clerk!" the foreman had thought, but Mother Wessels took him in with the warm, cordial hospitality characteristic of the true full-blooded Boer woman of the wild.

So he was sitting at the hearth, staring pensively into the leaping flames, and listening to the conversation. But he himself did not speak. Only his dry cough could be heard occasionally.

"And what do you say of this, Cousin?" asked Mother Wessels, who felt sorry that the stranger was not included in the conversation.

There followed a moment of silence. All eyes turned to the deep shadow. Wessels's sons could hardly contain their inquisitiveness and impatience.

"He's a Redneck!" whispered Karel to his brother Kees.

"Keep quiet," said Kees, afraid of missing a word, "and listen!"

"I agree with Master Wessels," said the stranger softly, "we don't know what the time is on God's world clock. But I don't doubt that we will have war."

"May God keep us from the terrors of war!" cried Mother Wessels, but her husband consoled her by saying, "Paul Kruger is in charge, and he is willing to pay a high price for peace."

"But surely he won't sacrifice the independence of the Republic for it, will he?" said the soft voice of the stranger.

"Unthinkable!" answered the man of the house emphatically. "He would much rather be hanged."

"Therefore there will be war," said the stranger calmly, "and quite soon too. And God will use England as a scourge to discipline the Boers!"

Everybody in the room looked up in shock, but old Wessels assented by nodding his graying head.

"There are grave national sins, and the gold has not done you much good. The nation has strayed from the good old ways," continued the stranger.

His words carried a serious reproach, but no one felt they could be angry with him. The soft friendliness of his tone disarmed them. But young Karel was squirming on his chair, more than ever convinced that they were dealing with a secret Redneck. For that was the belief of the British, that God used them to discipline the nations, and that He took the gold and diamonds from the godless nations and gave it to the good Englishmen.

"You can cut off my head if he is not a Redneck!" he said softly and emphatically to Kees, who gave no answer.

The stranger coughed, the same hoarse, dry cough as before, and continued, "There is still something else I would like to point out — the relationship between the Boers and the native blacks. I am in no position to judge anybody, but I would like to ask: Have not the Afrikaans Boers fallen short in their Christian vocation toward the blacks?"

Everybody, even Master Wessels, looked up in astonishment and stared at the deep shadow in which the figure of the strange man could only vaguely be seen. But Karel shook his younger brother by the sleeve with a feeling of definite triumph, and whispered: "What do you say now, Kees? That's what I said, 'Cut off my head if he is not a Redneck!' "

This time Karel was not alone. All the others were disturbed, even indignant, and even the soft friendly tone of the stranger could no longer disarm their anger.

"How long have you been staying among these people?" old Wessels asked. "Less than a year, you say? And from which sources have you formed your opinion on the native question? From the reports of the English missionaries?"

"Livingstone, Philips, and Moffat are my sources," answered the stranger.

"That's what I thought," sighed old Wessels; "the missionaries did us no good turn with their reports. They have to understand that we *cannot* treat the blacks as our equals."

"Not as equals, but as children," the stranger gave his opinion; "that is what God demands."

"And that is what we do," said old Wessels.

"But you don't allow them in your places of worship," added the stranger.

"That we *cannot* do," said Wessels, "for they would forget about the distance between them and us, that cannot be bridged on this side of the grave."

"Why can't it be bridged?" asked the stranger.

"Because the distance does not lie in the colour of their skin, but in the big difference in mental and spiritual capacity. The native question is a very sensitive and difficult question, on which most people coming from Europe can only pass a very shallow judgment. We Afrikaans Boers have been planted in this land as a government over these blind heathens to uphold the scales of sacred justice. That is our first calling."

"And to bring them the gospel," said the stranger.

"Of course!" said Wessels.

"And do your people fulfil this calling?" asked the stranger in his soft voice.

He seemed to be groping with his hands to find the shortcomings, the weaknesses, the sins of the Afrikaans people, and the man sitting next to him already had a sharp answer on his tongue.

But then the flames rose high in the fireplace, and the bright light they gave off chased away the shadows. The stranger could now be clearly seen; he was fully in the light.

He must have risen from his chair at his last words, since he was now standing upright and his gentle gaze went slowly from person to person. The sharp words died on Albert's lips, and the young Karel began to doubt that the young man really was an Englishman.

The face now visible was a narrow, pale, clean-shaven one. The eyes were deeply sunken, and on both cheeks a tell-tale red spot could be seen.

"A sure sign of death!" sighed Mother Wessels, and her gaze rested on the stranger, full of sympathy.

But since the others were keeping quiet, he went on, "I love this people, and my days are numbered — what else can I do but point out the existence of certain defects?"

"You seem to be a true Israelite in whom there is nothing false," said old Wessels with warmth in his voice; "and if it is love for my people that causes you to speak and warn us, then speak up freely any time!"

But Daniel had risen, and was now looking the consumptive man in the face with his tender-hearted gaze, asking in his appealing voice, "Do you love Jesus?"

"Yes," said the stranger, "I love Him very much. All who know Him, love him."

"Do you have relatives in this country?"

"I have neither brothers nor sisters, only a mother, who lives far from here — in Europe."

"And why did you not stay with your mother?" Daniel asked with quiet reproach.

"My lungs have been affected, and the doctor advised a stay in South Africa. I thought I would be able to pay my way by teaching, so I came."

He became sad as he said this, for he was thinking of his mother whom he would never see again. Daniel too, became sad and they both remained silent.

The fire in the hearth was dying down, and in the corner where the stranger sat, deep darkness reigned once more.

Daniel went to his mother and whispered, "Surely the stranger can stay here tonight?"

"Of course, my boy," answered his mother.

"How long can he stay, Mother?"

"For as long as you wish, Daniel!"

"Oh," said the boy. "Then he will stay for a long time!" And he kissed his mother.

But Aunt Sannie thought, "It will be five weeks at the most!" And Aunt Sannie was right.

Chapter III
Tricked

The dew was still on the fields when a horseman departed from *Wonderfontein* the following morning.

It was Louis, the young hunter.

He patted the shining neck of the bay on which he was mounted, and rode down the lane at a steady pace, afterward taking the main road. Pluto ran ahead, with huge elated bounds.

The previous night Louis had attentively followed the conversation on the war that was probably to break out, but it had not caused him to lose any sleep. On this quiet, lovely morning he felt like a playful young foal that had the freedom of the *veld*, or like the eagle rising above his head to the cloudless blue sky to hover above and bask in the first rays of the morning sun.

His contented gaze went over the lovely countryside. He greeted the fresh wildflowers, bright among the green grass, and he sang a hearty hunting song which resounded from the surrounding hills.

No wonder he was so light-hearted! Today he was on his way to visit his fiancee whom he was to marry in six weeks' time. The farm on which the young couple would live was ready, and the new house almost completed. The future lay ahead of the young hunter like a smiling Eden and neither cloud nor shadow darkened the sunlight shining on his path. His heart was full of hope and ideals, and standing on this mountain peak of his life, he felt light and nimble like the quick deer crossing the field about three hundred yards away.

Automatically he took the rifle from his shoulder, obeying his hunting instinct. Yet he did not take aim. This morning he could not bring himself to kill the noble animal.

"It wants to live and enjoy life — isn't its life short enough?" he thought to himself, and returned the rifle to his shoulder.

A hare jumped up from under his horse's hooves. Pluto was already pursuing the terrified animal at a fast pace, but the young hunter called back the dog, which searched his master's face with wide intelligent eyes, for this he could not understand.

After riding for about four hours he came to the river. There was a ford there, a shallow place where one could cross, but heavy rain had caused the river to swell unexpectedly, so that the ford was impassable.

But what did it matter? The young hunter took off his clothes, tied them on top of the saddle, and led the horse into the river. He had to swim to reach the other side. With his left hand Louis held onto his tail, and with his right hand he held his gun, a precious Henri-Martini rifle, above his head to prevent it from getting wet.

Without mishap horse and rider reached the opposite bank. On this side, in the vast *veld* not far from the ford, stood an inn, also the store, of Mr. Blijvenstein. It boasted a shabby iron sign on which was painted in bright red an unlikely snake with great wings, and under it the name: *The Flying Rattlesnake.*

The place stood near the main road, and since the transport riders on their long trips always unhitched their wagons there, and took on new stock of food and other necessities, Mr. Blijvenstein had a flourishing business. He sold nearly everything: shoes and salad oil, saddles and hake fish, dried apricots and tinned meat.

Louis Wessels walked across the wide yard, where an ostrich was pacing back and forth with long, careful steps, threw the reins of his horse to a young black man who had been lazing on the ground, and entered the inn.

It was a huge, bare, inhospitable room. There were a few shabby tables and some unpainted wooden benches. At the window, which overlooked the yard and the road, sat the owner of the establishment, Mr. Blijvenstein.

The man made an unfavourable first impression. His small gray eyes had something cunning and dishonest in them. They roved back and forth all the time, and never seemed to rest. His long body lounged on a chair with a cane seat, and his short legs rested on one of the long benches. His head was very large, and he did not seem to have any neck at all. His nearest relatives had long since reconciled themselves to the prospect of Uncle Jaap Blijvenstein passing away suddenly some day as a result of apoplexy.

It was said that he must have a good deal of money, lots and lots of it. But there was no one who knew how much he really had. It was true that he earned a lot from the travellers and transport riders, and equally true that he did not use correct weights and measures. That he constantly tricked coloured people and whites whenever he got the chance, was no less true.

There was an irritated expression on the inn-keeper's face as the young hunter entered. The day before his fifteen-year-old servant had run off. He was young Barend Klaassens, usually called Blikoortje because he had lived in the Free State for some time.

Blijvenstein was kicking angrily at the backrest of a bench with his short legs, thinking of the events of the day before. It really was an ugly business! Blikoortje had become more or less indispensable to his master Blijvenstein. He entertained the travellers in the inn with his jokes, and the transport riders who could not stand the miserly inn-keeper, bought more than they had intended to when clever Blikoortje was in the shop.

He knew something about everything. He could fix a torn saddle, serve customers in the shop, he knew the secret of healing the injured foot of an ox, and claimed to have a complete cure for every toothache. On top of this he was honest. Master Blijvenstein had gone through his pockets every night as the boy lay sleeping, and never found anything more than a few old buttons.

But the day before Blikoortje had suddenly left. That surely was a nasty business! Whatever happened?

Master Blijvenstein had no wife or children, but he had had an old black woman for a long time, who did the cooking and kept his house in order. But two days earlier he had given her the sack because she ate too much for his liking. The previous day, Blikoortje had had to act as cook. He had killed a couple of cockerels, roasted them, and dished them up to the master's liking, and the master had eaten them with relish. And of course Blikoortje had to be watching!

A few hours later, after having had his midday rest, Master Blijvenstein had walked through the yard. He was looking for his servant, and peered around the corner of the house. That was his usual way of searching. Spying had become part and parcel of this miserable man's life.

Behind the house in the cattle *kraal*, which was empty at the time, he had discovered his young servant. Blikoortje was sitting with his back against the low stone wall of the *kraal*, in the shadow. He was holding a huge plate between his brown hands and tucking in. The inn-keeper was almost positive that what he had on his plate were a couple of roasted cockerels.

But he had said nothing, and ran back to the chicken coop on his short legs to count his cockerels. He was quite at a loss, for he counted only two less than the day before. Then there had been fourteen, and now there were twelve. The missing two he, the master, had eaten himself. But where had the rascal gotten the chickens he was eating?

He had wrung his hands as his cunning little gray eyes roved around, searching and spying. He did not want to ask the boy himself for an explanation, for fear of being lied to. His huge head was confronted with an important and difficult question. But on the dung-heap lay the solution to the riddle. Jaap Blijvenstein's big hands trembled when he picked up the hide of a cat.

Livid with rage he had rushed on the young servant.

"Villain!" he roared. "Do you know this cat skin?"

"You give me a fright, Master," said Blikoortje, finishing off the last tasty bones.

"I ask you once more: Do you know this cat skin?"

"Let me have a look at it, Master," said the servant.

The master held the skin out to him, himself boiling inside.

The boy had carefully inspected the skin, both inside and out, licked his fingers, and then said with great confidence: "That is the hide of our tomcat, Saremie."

"And you have killed and eaten this cat," roared the inn-keeper of *The Flying Rattlesnake*. "I thought you had chickens on your plate, but it was my cat — my little pussy — you vulgar beast!"

"Oh, I haven't eaten the cat," the boy assured him, rising just as a precaution.

"So then, who *has*?" railed the old man.

What evil and perverse spirit took possession of young Blikoortje is difficult to tell, yet he spoke the truth when he said: "You, Master Blijvenstein — you have eaten the cat. I don't like pussycats — I eat chickens if I can get them."

The inn-keeper was convinced that the villain was speaking the truth and had served him up the cat, and then finished off the juicy cockerels. As a matter of fact, he *had* been surprised by the extraordinary bone structure of the chickens!

He was gasping for breath. His swollen face became blue with anger, and he stretched out his rough hands to catch the scoundrel. But he tripped over a ladder lying at his feet, and fell down on his face at full length.

The servant had used this moment to rush into the house, grab his clothes and other possessions and run off. He had escaped through the back door just as the master entered through the front door.

However, by then the master's anger had cooled considerably, and he realized that he couldn't, at least not at that busy time, do without his young servant. So when he hadn't found the boy inside, he had gone out again, calling in his friendliest voice, "Blikoortje! Come here, my boy!"

"What?" replied the boy, feeling he had the upper hand, now that he had his possessions under his arm.

"I'll forgive you," declared the old man with a smile. "Just carry on with your work, my boy!"

"What will you forgive — that I, just like the old black woman, have so often gone hungry in your house?"

The inn-keeper's blood was rising to his head once more.

"You are an obstinate brute!" he burst out.

"And you are an ugly, stingy thickhead!" mocked Blikoortje, and disappeared.

He was stingy, was Master Blijvenstein, that was certain. When he could not sleep at night he would get up, light a tallow candle, and count his riches. It was the greatest pleasure he knew. How the silver coins jingled against each other! How the gold shone! He would count and recount the same bag four or five times. And he never tired of counting it, for the counting seemed to hold a strange, fascinating spell over him. He would have liked to go on counting, day and night, workdays and Sundays, summer and winter, going on and on . . . He could even reconcile himself with the coffin in the end, if only it had room to count . . .

But a coffin is narrow, and affords little room. Master Blijvenstein knew that too, and therefore he feared death. A slight indisposition would make him positively ill, and he had a definite dislike of people who spoke about death and eternity.

Louis Wessels knew Master Blijvenstein quite well. He was surprised that Blikoortje was not to be seen, and the inn-keeper told him in full detail what a mean trick the boy had played on him.

The young hunter had a hearty laugh.

"That's just the type of thing for Blikoortje to do," he said, then ordered bread and milk and ate to his heart's content, for the long ride had given him an appetite.

"I suppose the journey is to Natal?" said the inn-keeper, who knew that Louis Wessels's fiancee lived in Natal.

"Good guess!" he answered with a laugh. He glanced at his watch, and, asking the inn-keeper to look after his horse during his absence, walked to the little railway station which was situated half an hour's walk farther, standing all by itself on the endless prairie.

Chapter IV
Annoyances

The sun was at its highest point, at midday, and it was sweltering hot. The heat was especially noticeable near a flat area where there were no trees or shrubs. It was a platform, belonging to one of the railway stations of the Northern Natal Railway line linking Natal with Transvaal. Because of the glowing heat, it was dead quiet. There was a black porter with a trunk at the station, and a few geese crossed the platform to visit a muddy ditch. That was all.

But on the dirt road a girl was nearing the platform on horseback. A broad-brimmed hat covered her long, chestnut brown hair. She could not have been much more than nineteen years old. A black man, also on horseback, was following her at a distance.

When she reached the platform, she dismounted, while the black man, a young, slender Zulu with intelligent black eyes, followed her example. She looked at her watch, and then gazed down the railway line to the north to see if she could see the steam of the approaching train.

However, she saw nothing. Somewhat disappointed, she took the reins and her riding-whip in her left hand while with her right hand she chased away the flies humming about the head of her dappled gray mount. Every now and then she would look out toward the north, but whatever she was waiting for did not seem to be coming.

"When is your future master coming?" she whispered in the ear of her small sturdy horse, but he shook his head as if to say, "How should I know?"

She stood shifting impatiently about on her small feet, and after having waited for about ten minutes, called, "Christiaan!"

By "Christiaan" she meant the young Zulu who was holding his big dark brown horse.

She gave him the reins of her pony and went up the platform toward the station. A guard was walking down the line to check the switches. On the platform stood the stationmaster and a railway clerk talking.

"When will the Transvaal train finally be coming?" asked the girl.

"She's on her way, Miss!" the stationmaster greeted the girl, who was known to him.

"It is a quarter of an hour late already!" And she pointed with her riding-whip at the station clock which stood at one o'clock.

"Not quite — only seven minutes," the stationmaster laughed. "You are extraordinarily impatient today, Miss Uys!"

"Love makes one impatient," rejoined the scrawny clerk, turning his neck, which looked like a long dried beanstalk.

Then the electric bell rang, and in the distance a plume of steam from the approaching train could be seen.

"Nowadays not much good comes out of the Transvaal," joked the stationmaster.

"But for me, something very good!" said the girl looking up frankly with her clear blue eyes.

"Take care that you remain a faithful subject of our queen!" the stationmaster laughed, lifting a warning finger.

But she did not hear these last words since her attention was wholly fixed on the train which was steaming into the station. The doors were thrown open and a stream of passengers poured out.

There were all kinds of people: old gentlemen with gold-rimmed spectacles on their noses and half-naked blacks; a cavalry officer with a long sabre next to a beggar with a wooden leg. And everybody seemed to be in a hurry. People are always in a hurry! They rush from home to the railway station, and the train is much too slow; and they rush from the station home again, always going to and fro, until between their home and the station they tumble into a grave and remain there, lying still.

But the young girl had no time to reflect on these matters. Her eyes were searching for her bridegroom-to-be among the bustling and scurrying people. She did not have to search for long. For there he was — the one with the cheerful face. But why was he not making more haste in reaching her?

Then she saw why. He was helping a woman with her luggage, an old lady shrivelled with age.

Yes, it was so true to his nature: always helpful. Was that any reason to be irritated? The slight cloud lifted from her brow. "He is better than I am," she thought.

But now the old lady did not need his help any longer, and the young man was also hurrying.

"Truida!" he called.

"Louis! Welcome!"

The words were few, but they chased the last shadows of irritation from Truida's face. In the tone in which they pronounced each other's name was expressed all the sincerity, tenderness, and fondness of their love. There was nothing insincere, pretentious, or strained in their greeting. Unnecessary it was too, for true love brings simplicity.

They went quickly through the waiting room of the station. Christiaan had already brought the horses to the front entrance by the path flagged with blue stone. Truida took the pony. The brown horse was intended for Louis.

The horses had already become impatient and were pawing the ground. Both young people mounted and gave the horses full rein.

The stationmaster and the scrawny clerk followed them with their eyes.

"A fine-looking couple!" was the stationmaster's comment.

"He looks impudent enough!" said the clerk.

"They won't ask you to the wedding," said the stationmaster.

"There won't be a wedding," rejoined the thin man.

"In six weeks' time, my friend!"

"Oh no, they'll quarrel before then. He is a Transvaal Boer, and she has been to an English boarding school. I needn't say any more."

"And if it falls through, you will marry the rich Miss Uys," jeered the stationmaster.

"She could do worse!" commented the scrawny clerk, and he gave his thin neck such a turn that it began creaking in an ominous way.

The young pair had a long ride ahead of them, but it was a beautiful sunny day and they were in no hurry. At least they were together now. But it troubled Louis Wessels that they repeatedly came across English cavalry.

"I believe you would prefer to not see them, Louis."

"I really am surprised, Truida, the place is swarming with Rednecks."

"But they were here before," she laughed.

"Not so many of them. I have seen them everywhere now — at Laingsnek, at Newcastle, at Glencoe — literally everywhere!"

"As a rule you are somewhat forward," Truida joked, "so that's why they are taking precautions."

At that moment a full field battery came around the bend at a gallop, and the young couple had to be quick not to be run over. The barrels of the rifles shone brightly, and the drawn sabres flashed in the sunlight.

A frown formed between the Boer's eyes. He was staring at the shining artillery with a stern face. He followed them with his eyes until they disappeared in a cloud of dust. It looked as if a vision was hovering before his inner eye.

"Come along!" called the girl, and with a laugh she flicked Wessels's horse with her riding-whip so that he sprang forward. They resumed their journey, but Louis was silent. He seemed to have been affected by the sight of the cannon.

"Surely you have seen British artillery before?" Truida asked, a little disconcerted now.

"Of course," he said; "at Krugersdorp, for instance!"

Krugersdorp — she thought it unkind of him to remind her of Krugersdorp, where the unfortunate Jameson had gambled away his cannon, his men, and his freedom. She was not pro-Transvaal, true; but could Louis hold it against her? She had been born in a colony to parents who were subjects of Queen Victoria, and she had been taught in the boarding school in Pietermaritzburg (the scrawny railway clerk had been right) that South Africa as a whole would only flourish once it had been firmly allied with the British Empire.

"I don't think it is nice of you to speak of Krugersdorp, Louis," she said, "for Krugersdorp was a prank, and England was innocent of it."

"Innocent!" he exclaimed in a bitter tone. "Innocent!" He pulled at the reins so that his horse reared wildly.

She had never seen him so upset, and she looked at him in growing astonishment.

"Krugersdorp was a misunderstanding — a terrible misunderstanding."

"That's what those Jingoistic English papers make of it," he answered angrily, "but that is a lie — for it was a carefully planned, a devilish plan to snatch Naboth's vineyard. But the Afrikaans Naboth was more fortunate on New Year's Day of 1896 than the Naboth of 1 Kings 21, and if Cronjé had not been so swift to react,

England would have taken the whole of Transvaal — of course under a mere misunderstanding."

He said this with a laugh, but it wasn't the old, jovial laugh, and looking at him closely, Truida guessed that something definite must have happened.

"Have matters become tense?" she asked.

"War is looming," he said. "I don't doubt that any longer. The conference at Bloemfontein has come to nothing, and England is amassing its soldiers here in Natal — doesn't that mean war?"

"I haven't heard about a failed conference."

"I have the paper in my pocket. You can read it later on," he answered.

"But surely it need not lead to war," she exclaimed in alarm.

"If England keeps up its demands, there *will* be war, Truida!"

"But then it will be the fault of the Boers."

"Why is that?" he asked in surprise.

"Well, if they would give in, everything would be all right."

"Yes, of course — if they are willing to bow down before England, they will be allowed to live."

"It's only about the rights of the *uitlanders*, Louis."

"It's about our existence as a nation, Truida. I am surprised that you don't understand *that*!"

No, she did not understand that; she had never understood it. But she was sincere in her opinion that the Boers were narrow-minded and conservative in denying the *uitlanders* their due rights, and young Wessels was too embittered to unravel the lies from the truth by calmly explaining the matter to her.

Pluto shot forward and stood barking at a little dog that belonged to one of the blacks, who was lying on the road with a piece of meat between its forelegs. As Pluto was hungry, he decided to take the enticing piece of meat for himself. He laid down flat on his stomach, sniffing the delicious aroma, and then jumped up again, and began to bark loudly.

"Pluto — come here!" Truida called.

"Why do you call back my dog?" asked Louis.

"Don't you see that he wants to take away the little dog's meat from him?" she asked in surprise.

"So what if he does, Truida?"

"What if he does? Why, it is theft — no, even worse — it is plain robbery!"

British soldiers leaving Southhampton

"And if England wants to have the gold mines — what is that?" he asked sharply.

"That is a different matter," she said.

"A different matter," he mocked. "Oh well, let's not speak about it anymore!"

Truida now felt truly offended. She did not reply, and they both rode on in silence. The blue corrugated iron roof of Truida's home could already be seen through the trees, and they had come to the end of their journey.

Chapter V
A Close Encounter

Truida grew pale as they came into the yard, and the frown deepened on Louis' forehead.

"Whose horses are these?" he asked in a loud voice of the servants holding the reins of a number of cavalry horses. It was an unnecessary question. He could see whose horses they were from the saddles and other equipment.

"I thought as much," he mumbled when the oldest servant answered, "They belong to British officers."

With feminine intuition Truida feared an awkward incident, and whispered, "Wait a little, Louis — they are bound to leave soon!"

Her intentions were good, but Louis was in a very irritated mood, and all afternoon he had been interpreting everything in a negative way.

"So you suggest I should remain outside while the great British officers are inside?" he demanded. "Not a chance!" he continued angrily as he made for the front door. She had no choice but to follow him, but her heart was pounding. Together they entered the living room.

Some seven officers — dragoons and lancers — were seated there, with glasses of wine in front of them on the table, while the host, Arend Uys, Truida's father, sat in the corner next to the fireplace.

He got up when the young couple entered, welcomed young Wessels cordially, inquired how his family was, and told the officers that this young man was to be his son-in-law.

Master Uys was very pleased with his future son-in-law. He was a practical old farmer, and could see that his beloved child would be well off with such a husband. Truida was his only child, and her mother had passed away at her birth. An old aunt had come to keep house for him after his wife's death; thus the complete family consisted of only three persons.

The exchange with her father made Truida feel more relaxed. One could not say that Louis' attitude toward the officers was cordial, but he was not uncivil either, and when Pluto made a nuisance of himself by sniffing at all the officers, he was obliging enough to take his dog outside.

Master Uys was in a very good mood today. He had received an exceptionally high price for his wool, and the officers, who were never shy about helping themselves, complimented him by saying that no one else had such good wine in his cellar. There was in fact some truth in it. He had the best wine, and the best sheep, within twenty miles, though one would not suppose this simple farmer with his shabby hat, working clothes, and short stone pipe to be a rich landowner.

He never spoke about politics and no one knew which party he belonged to. Once Louis had tried to speak to him on the subject as they were walking through the beautiful orchard behind the house.

"Now is the time for a free, united South Africa," Louis had said.

Master Uys had taken him by the arm, pointing to a peach tree nearby. "Pick a peach," the old farmer had said.

"That would be a pity," Louis had replied.

"Why would it be a pity, Louis?"

"Because the peach is not ripe yet, Uncle!"

"Exactly," Master Uys had declared. "There is a time for everything on earth — for the fruit to form on the trees, for the fruit to ripen, and for the fruit to be picked."

And with this he had gone away and driven off an ostrich which had escaped from its pen.

And just a short while ago, a vehement Jingoist had spoken to him about politics and the necessity of incorporating Transvaal, which posed an imminent threat to the authority of England.

But Master Uys had called one of his oldest servants and had asked him, "Manasse, tell me, why have you served me faithfully for forty years?"

"Oh, Master," Manasse had replied, "when I came to you with my young child, ill, helpless, and destitute, you did not set your dogs on me the way your neighbour had done, but you have been to me and my child like an angel of God. You have won Manasse's heart, and that's why Manasse serves you."

"See? You must first win the hearts of the Boers," Master Uys had said to the Jingoist, "and everything else will fall in place!"

On hearing these words the man had shrugged with contempt — what did he care for the hearts of the Boers? It was their gold he wanted — just their gold . . .

Truida had gone off to see to the supper, and Christiaan had called his old master to see to an ox that was sick. Thus the British officers stayed behind with the young Boer. They had made substantial inroads into Master Uys's store of wine and were all talking loudly. At most there were two who had remained sober. One officer with an enormous black moustache now stood up, filled the glasses once more, and called out in a powerful voice: "To a favourable outcome, friends! In Pretoria within six weeks!"

The glasses clinked against each other. Only one glass remained untouched.

"Come on, Mr. Wessels, drink with us," said the man with the black moustache.

"What am I to drink to?"

"To a favourable outcome — in Pretoria within six weeks!"

"The only way I can drink to that," said Louis, "is if it means that within six weeks you will be in Pretoria as a prisoner of war."

This simple speech had a peculiar effect. Had a bomb fallen in the room the British could not have been more astounded. However, their astonishment lasted only a few seconds, to be replaced by unbounded contempt.

"I suppose you are one of Paul Kruger's paid spies?" commented the moustache impudently.

The only reply Louis made was to get up, turn his back to the company, and look out the window. He could have gone out, of course, but considered it beneath his dignity to do so.

"How much do you get?" asked a brawny fellow, generally known as Mad Max.

Louis did turn around for a moment then. He folded his arms and said with bitter scorn, "And they call these British officers!"

For a moment silence reigned, and then one of the two sober officers, a young man of noble appearance, aired the thought that it was time to go.

"But I still want to know how much he gets paid for spying!" said Mad Max, pointing to the young Boer who was staring out of the window, having turned his back on them again.

"Hey, lad," he called, making a sign with his thumb and forefinger which could not be misconstrued, "how much of this do you get?"

Louis remained motionless. It was only when the black moustache said, "He is of the same calibre as his boss Master Kruger, who is a foolish baboon!" that he turned around again. It cost him the utmost effort to practice self-restraint. It looked like he was still calm, but he was as white as the whitewashed wall behind him.

He took a quick stride to the table where the officers sat drinking, and crashed his hard farmer's fist on the table so that the wine glasses clattered. The frown on his forehead had deepened to an ominous thundercloud.

"Who dares to call Paul Kruger a foolish baboon?" he cried in a hoarse voice.

"I do!" roared the black moustache.

"And I — and I — and I!" shouted three more officers.

"And how would you gentlemen like it if I called Queen Victoria a foolish baboon?" he demanded.

"Such impudence would naturally be punished with a whip!" answered the moustache.

"With a whip!" repeated the mad one. It was clear that these men were doing their utmost to provoke a quarrel with the Boer.

"With the whip?" the young hunter repeated slowly. He cast his eye over the room. In one corner stood the sturdy riding-whip where Truida had put it down.

He took it up. His muscular hand gripped it firmly. Twice it whistled through the air with such unrelenting force that it raised a livid cross on the face of the officer with the black moustache.

All the officers jumped up as if they had been bitten by a tarantula.

"Look! Look! That's how it is!" jeered the young hunter with cutting contempt. "Seven officers against one Boer — then they have courage!"

He was somehow relieved that the storm had broken loose. The muscles in his arms became as hard as steel. He took his stand in the corner of the room, pushing the table in front of him as a barricade, and took a chair in each hand.

In the meantime the officers had drawn their sabres.

"We will thrash the rascal!" said one of the young officers, but he received such a hard blow in the chest with the leg of the chair that he fell down. Three officers yanked at the chair Louis held in his left hand, and soon he was left with nothing more than a piece of the back, which he whacked to pieces on the heads of his opponents.

"Artillery — fire!" shouted the mad one, and the others followed his example, taking the empty wine bottles from the table to bombard the young hunter with them. Just as the wild fellow, armed with two empty bottles, was about to begin the barrage, he happened to glance sideways toward the door. Shamefacedly he dropped the bottles. His comrade next to him, who had just unhooked his sabre to throw it at the head of the young Boer, grew pale.

In the doorway stood the major!

How long had he been there? Who could say? Quite possibly he had been there for a quarter of an hour, and had heard and seen it all.

He stood there, cool and collected, motionless as a statue, his hand on the hilt of his sword.

Only too well did they know him — he was strict and relentless! He had been against the promotion of his own son, a young lieutenant, because he was of the opinion that his son had not deserved the promotion.

So there he stood, in the doorway, like the law in stone. Under his cold, severe look the brawlers miraculously became immediately sober.

Louis could see that he had been rescued, and slowly pushed aside the table. In amazement he stared at the small major with the gray hair, wondering how this incident would end.

But nothing extraordinary happened.

The officers stood there like criminals conscious of their deeds before a judge, and at this moment they were indeed making a poor impression. Only Mad Max had recovered enough from his fright to be able to whisper in the ear of the moustache: "Thank the Transvaal rogue for the two blue welts — the major won't recognize you. At the moment you look exactly like an orangutang!"

But the major did recognize him. Slowly he put his hand in his shirt-pocket and took out his little black notebook. And he deliberately wrote down the names of the officers — one by one — with torturing calm. Then he stepped aside from the doorway, and made way for them to exit. They had to go right past the small dreaded man, and they felt like schoolboys caught stealing apples.

When the last one had departed, the major followed. The young hunter stayed behind alone, among pieces of broken glass and chair legs. His first fight with the British seemed like a dream to him.

But it wasn't a dream — when Truida came in she saw at a glance that something terrible had happened.

"I was afraid of this," she said.

"Well, I could not back down before the officers," he said in his old jocular tone.

"You should have listened to me, my dear," she said affectionately, "and waited a while until they had gone."

"But you yourself would have thought that cowardly, Truida, wouldn't you?"

It was true. She would have thought him lacking in courage if he had stayed outside because of the British cavalry officers. It was only through anxiety for him that she had given the advice which she knew in her heart he could not have followed.

"Have my countrymen dealt mercifully with you?" she asked, while looking him over with some concern.

"Your *countrymen* would have liked to thrash me," he said, "but they were not given the chance."

He was irritated that she called the officers her countrymen. Truida could tell by the tone of his voice. It saddened her, and her clear blue eyes filled with tears.

"We don't seem to understand each other today," she said, "and I have been looking forward to this day with so much joy."

This complaint touched his soul, for he truly loved her.

"Forgive me," he said sincerely, "if I have hurt you. I've seen so many British uniforms today that I am irritable, dear Truida!"

"The Transvaal question need not cloud our relationship," she replied, lifting her fair face to him, now lit up by the setting sun.

"No," he said with warmth and endearment, "that's true — come Trui! I must still see your flowers and your shrubs and your beautiful birds, and we will shelve the Afrikaans question."

It was once more his old familiar tone and Truida cheered up. The clouds lifted from his face like mist before the morning sun, and Truida's eyes rested once more on the sunny, friendly face she loved.

Hand in hand they went outside to the flower garden. Roses filled the air with their fragrance, and tulips swayed gently in the evening breeze. And Truida had to tell the young hunter all the little secrets which she had saved for him, and he listened with rivetted attention, though they were mere trifles. They laughed and joked as of old. They enjoyed the warmth of one another's love and were as happy as children with no worries.

They walked among the flower beds, three, four times, then across the yard to the extensive orchard, sitting down under a spreading plum tree. In the branches a bird was singing and they listened to its beautiful evening song.

It was late by the time they went inside. The stars were out, and over the hills the moon was rising. At the door stood the old aunt, the housekeeper, waiting for the young couple.

"Have you heard?" asked the garrulous old woman. "Have you heard? We will be having British troops here! They'll be billeted with us!"

With one blow the old wound was ripped open again.

"Who told you that?" Louis asked.

"Well, a soldier brought a note. There is nothing we can do about it. Oh my! We live in sad times, Cousin! This afternoon they smashed everything in our living room to smithereens, and who knows, Cousin, what's to come! The night before last I saw a snake in the air, a great, terrifying, fiery snake, Cousin, and the dogs would not be pacified; and last night I saw in a dream nothing but burning butter kegs, Cousin . . ."

"Yes, yes! It is as you say!" Louis said shortly, and went into the house.

He had a faint hope that the billeting would prove not to be true, but Master Uys looked more serious than usual when he said, "It is so. They will be here tomorrow already!"

Chapter VI
The Broken Bond

Louis Wessels did not sleep a wink all night, and Truida looked paler than usual when she appeared at the breakfast table.

Little was said at the table, except by the housekeeper who, true to her habit, chattered on and on.

The table was cleared and old Master Uys, filling his little stone pipe, went outside to see to his livestock. He was not turned from his normal habits and took everything with amazing calmness. Under that well-worn and faded waistcoat there lurked a heart full of imperturbable wisdom. If at that moment his beautiful house had taken fire, he would still have said, "Be still; everything will work out all right!"

But young Wessels had not reached that stage yet, and his heart was full of anxiety. Until recently he had lived under the illusion that should a war break out, South Africa, from Table Bay to the Zambezi, would rise as one man against British violence, but his expectations had lessened considerably in the last few days. On his journey he had noticed that the Dutch-Afrikaans part of Natal on the whole wished for victory for their race in Transvaal, but that it would for the time being remain no more than a wish.

It really should not have been surprising. Even his soon-to-be father-in-law was of the opinion that the time had not yet come for one unified Afrikaans empire which could stand on its own. And as far as Truida was concerned . . . she had just entered the room, and now took a chair near him.

"You didn't sleep well," she said in a calm and friendly voice.

"And you have been crying," he answered in his old cordial tone.

"You said you would shelve the Afrikaans question," she said in a weak effort to smile, but her lips were trembling.

"I *cannot!*" he sighed.

"Why can't you, Louis?"

"Because God has planted deep in my soul a love for our national independence, Truida."

"But surely our independence will not be threatened even if the *uitlanders are* given a five-year vote?"

"It is not a matter of the vote — it is about the gold mines, about Naboth's vineyard! Naboth must die, because the vineyard belongs to him!"

Truida did not reply immediately, for she was engaged in an inner struggle. Then she looked up again, and asked quietly, "What do you expect from me?"

"That you will side with what is fair and right!"

"You mean side with the Boers?"

"Of course!" he said. "For they have justice on their side."

"But I say I *cannot* side with the Boers," she said in a steady voice.

Taken aback, he sought her eyes. "And why not?"

"Because I am a subject of the British queen."

"And have been to an English boarding school where the truth was turned around!" he said in anger.

"You are becoming very sharp and bitter, Louis," she said. "Please give me a chance to explain to you."

"I'm listening."

"I hope that war may still be avoided by the wisdom of politicians on both sides, but if war does break out, it will be a war between England and the Transvaal, and not between England and South Africa."

"And what about the Free State?" Louis asked in amazement.

"Well, then it will be a war between England and the two Boer republics, since the Free State will call down misery on themselves just for the sake of Transvaal. But the dream and the ideal of a United South Africa cannot be realized in this way."

"But in what way will it be realized otherwise?" he asked, his amazement increasing.

"Two years ago Natal, the Cape Colony, and the Free State took the first step to reach a South African customs union, but they were thwarted by the Transvaal's unwillingness."

"And why was the Transvaal unwilling, Truida?"

"I don't know," she said, shrugging her shoulders.

"Because one of Transvaal's conditions was a sea port, which England withheld from her in an unlawful manner. Without a port Transvaal would have had the bad end of the stick in such a customs union."

"We people from Natal also want an independent and united South Africa," said Truida, ignoring his last remark, "but we would resent being dominated by Pretoria just as much as by London."

So, that was it! It wounded his ardent soul — that jealousy, jealousy between people of the same race! Such jealousy, such distrust eroded their strength and made them defenceless against the powerful enemy. And as long as that worm of pettiness and envy gnawed at the race of the Dutch-Afrikaans people, there would be no growth or prosperity.

"Truida," he said, raising his voice, "as long as Natal fears that Pretoria may gain superiority, and the Cape Colony fears that Bloemfontein may gain superiority, and Ephraim envies Judah and Judah threatens Ephraim, we will have no strength. I'm afraid the day is still far off on which we will be able to speak of a free South African Commonwealth, of an empire on whose gates are written in gold letters: 'Righteousness exalts a nation, but sin is a disgrace to any people.' "

"A beautiful motto," she said; "but would you want to erect such a glorious building on a foundation of iniquity and sin?"

Her voice carried grave reproach as she said this, but Louis shook his head for he didn't understand her.

"You want the people of Natal," she continued, "to take up their rifles and take your side in the coming war?"

"Of course," Louis answered, "but it saddens me more than I can express to you, that I don't expect it to happen. A few courageous men will join us, but the greater part will remain at home."

"Fortunately!"

"Why fortunately?"

"Because it will prevent them from breaking their oath to our queen."

"Queen Victoria has a warm champion in you, the daughter of a Dutch Afrikaner!" said Louis not without bitterness.

"Should we rise against our lawful government?" she countered. Her cheeks were turning red, and her train of thought reflected the sharp brain she had inherited from her father.

"I will answer you," he said confidently. "As long as nations are underage they need a guardian, but when they have come of age, the yoke of guardianship should be lifted. England is the guardian to the South African colonies, but the child has grown to be a man, capable of directing his own affairs. It no longer needs to be ruled from a distance of more than six thousand miles. It is now a major."

Truida was about to reply, but at that moment the old housekeeper entered, looking upset. She shifted a vase that was perfectly well placed, and dusted a cupboard on which there was not a trace of dust.

She untied the strings of her black bonnet, refastened them with hands trembling with rage, and with her big slippers kicked at Pluto, who showed every intention of biting her in the leg. Then she set her pudgy hands on her hips, looked sharply at Truida, and said, "Trui, shouldn't you be helping me? Must I do *everything*? I'm only one person! I can't do everything! And say, Cousin, couldn't you keep this ugly mongrel beside you? I can't stand that animal with his blood-red eyes . . . What's the matter, Christiaan? Another accident?"

Christiaan brought the news that a lieutenant with ten lancers of the fifth had arrived and demanded that the men and horses be put up.

Truida looked at Louis on hearing this message, but the latter got up, seemingly undisturbed, called his dog and went out to the *veld*.

At the message brought by Christiaan the old housekeeper fell into a chair as if in a daze, and Truida had to arrange lodging for the lancers, which, in the light of Louis' present mood, was doubly unpleasant. But she was a brave, determined girl who could take matters in hand, and as it was a spacious house, everything was soon settled.

Louis did not return until midday. Truida was friendly and open, but he said little, which hurt her so that she also fell silent.

The rest of the day passed with its usual activities. Louis had gone off again, wanting to avoid meeting with the British lancers. Although Truida did not know this for sure, she did suspect it.

It was dusk by the time Louis turned up again. Truida was alone in the living-room and saw him approaching. He walked with a slight stoop, like someone in deep thought, and his dog was following him quietly. Heavy clouds filled the sky, and on the horizon the first lightning could be seen.

"You're just in time. There's a storm coming," said Truida, going out to meet him.

"I felt the first drops already," said Louis, sitting down beside her.

"Where is your father?" he asked after a short pause.

"He went to visit Kremer. The storm will overtake him."

Once more the conversation faltered.

From the adjoining room came the loud voices of the lancers. Truida would willingly have paid a great deal if she could have stopped their foul mouths, but she was helpless in that respect.

"Don't take any notice!" she said softly, pointing to the room.

"Never mind!" he said with a strange lightheartedness, and then was silent again. For Truida the silence was oppressive.

It was now possible to hear the soldiers clearly. They had just come from Pietermaritzburg where their garrison had been stationed, and had just settled the important question as to which bar in Pietermaritzburg sold the best whiskey. From whiskey they proceeded to the topic of the future — the expected war and the Boers. They did not expect a long war. After the second defeat the Boers would definitely go home — miserable cowards that they were!

"Don't take any notice!" Truida pleaded.

"Never mind!" he answered with icy calm, but a flash of lightning lit up his face and she saw that there was not a drop of blood in it.

"I will light the lamp," said Truida, but he laid a heavy hand on her arm.

"Don't," he said quietly. "We have to speak to each other."

Speak to each other — in such aggravating circumstances? Truida began to tremble. But the way he said it allowed no opposition. In her heart Truida prayed to God that her father would be home soon.

But her father stayed away.

Now the soldiers were talking even louder than before. They seemed to have become excited, and were holding forth with mockery and contempt over the Transvaal and its government.

"Well then, speak!" said Truida, who could stand the tension no longer.

"When are we going to be married, Truida?"

It was not the voice of a groom-to-be that she heard.

"You know that quite well," she said; "you do not need to ask me."

"Many things can happen before then," he said.

She made no reply — did she bear the responsibility for this war?

"And even if no war breaks out, I still couldn't live in Natal, as long as it is a British colony."

"You had no objection before," she said. "Have you suddenly changed your mind?"

"I could never bear to have British soldiers billeted in my house," he replied in a loud voice.

She made no answer.

In her heart she seemed to hear a small voice whispering, "He no longer loves you."

At this thought her eyes became devoid of emotion, and she felt fear in her heart beating wildly.

"Let us go and live in theTransvaal," he said. "I cannot submit myself to the British yoke — I would rather die!"

"He no longer loves you!" the voice in her heart whispered with a little more conviction.

"I am not going to the Transvaal," she suddenly said emphatically. "I shall stay in Natal."

He made no immediate reply. From the adjoining room could clearly be heard the coarse voice of a soldier shouting: "What shall we do with the fine president of Transvaal? We'll put him in an iron cage, and charge sixpence for people to see him at the fairs!"

Loud roars of laughter followed.

"Choose between me and Natal!" cried young Wessels in a voice hoarse with passion, anger, and pain.

He stood up, and so did Truida.

"Don't be tyrannized!" cried, no, shouted, the voice in her heart.

"I shall stay in Natal," she said in a cool, resolute tone.

He grabbed his hat.

"Is that your last word?" he said slowly. "You choose Natal over me?"

She made no reply, and he expected none.

"Come, Pluto," he said. "We have nothing more to say here!" and he exited hastily from the room and the house.

As the door closed behind the young hunter with a loud bang, Truida suddenly came to her senses. She did not share his opinions, but she could understand his reaction. She understood something of the passion raging in his honest heart for the freedom of his people, and the outrageous remarks of the arrogant lancers must have wounded him deeply.

She wanted to jump up and run after him. But she felt as if her whole body was broken, and she sank into a chair. But that was only for a fleeting moment. Then she did get up and ran out the door.

In the yard she hesitated for a moment, and then hurried down the lane to the main road. There she called out the name of her beloved, but her voice was lost in the power of the storm raging over the *veld*, and in the thunder which caused the mountains of Natal to tremble.

The rain lashed her face. She peered fearfully into the thick darkness. Suddenly a streak of lightning struck a cypress tree near her, and in the light she caught a glimpse of him approaching. Her heart lurched into her throat, and her burning eyes once more tried to pierce the palpable dark. She stood waiting and called, "Louis, here I am — Louis!"

A warm hand came down on her shoulder, and a voice full of compassion said, "It is not Louis, my child!"

Then she realized it was her father.

"Come back to the house, my little girl," he said sympathetically, "and tell me what has happened."

So together they came home.

The old housekeeper had lit the lamp and gone to bed, but father and daughter stayed up. And old Arend Uys brought his daughter a footstool, and once again she sat at his knees as she did in the days when he called her his dear little girl, and he let her speak her heart and cry. He did not interrupt her, but now and then his hand would go out with the love of a father to her thick chestnut hair. No one would have suspected such tenderness in this quiet man, but he loved his daughter, and love makes one tender. And when she had finished speaking and lifted her teary eyes to her father, he took his little girl's face in his huge rough hands, and said softly and comfortingly, "You have told your sorrows to your father on earth — now go and tell them to your heavenly Father! And then go to bed, my little girl, for you'll see — everything will work out all right!"

Chapter VII
Highwaymen

"Everything will work out all right" — could that possibly be true? With long strides Louis Wessels was making his way. At that particular moment it would have been difficult for him to believe that everything would work out all right. The storm was raging around him with unabated force, roaring rebellion with thunder and lightning. Nature seemed to reflect the storminess of his own heart, and the rain coming down hard and unmercifully in his face, felt good to him. Now and then he was blinded by the lightning and he would bump into a tree or a bush, or stumble into one of the deep potholes which abounded on the badly-made Afrikaans roads. But he paid no attention and was hardly worried about that, now that on the road of his life there was a pit that could not be bridged.

Pluto was walking ahead of the lonely traveller. He whined softly as if to show sympathy for his master, and barked whenever they came to a deep hole. But his master did not spare him an approving look, and the animal hung his big hairy head despondently.

Louis had been walking for a few hours. The thunderstorm and the rain had subsided significantly, and here and there between the drifting storm clouds a friendly star was twinkling. Now he could see better, and his trained hunter's eye discerned a shadow in the distance, which infuriated the dog, but Louis calmly went on.

He was now quite near the shadow standing in the middle of the road. When he looked back he could see a second shadow approaching him quickly from behind.

"Highwaymen!" was the young hunter's thought, and indeed he was right. But he had come across such men before. In places where there is gold, there is no lack of highwaymen, either great or small. He calmly continued on his way but they caught hold of him.

"Quiet, Pluto!" he said to the dog, who was threatening to take them by the throat. "Quiet!"

Then he addressed his attackers. "Let me go, and tell me what you want!"

He said this in curt, imperative tones, and the highwaymen realized that he wasn't afraid of the iron-studded cudgels in their hands. Perhaps they had not yet been practising this trade for long. At any rate, they actually let go of him momentarily.

"Hand over your purse," said the one thief, "and we will let you go!"

"We want his watch and his ring also, Bob!" said the second, whose name was Jim.

"Do you need anything else?" asked Louis calmly.

"I believe, Sir, that you are wearing a beautiful pair of long boots — I could make very good use of them, Sir!" said Jim.

"And my hat is very shabby," said Bob.

"Sir is also wearing a nice jacket," said Jim.

"Would you have me go without a jacket in this weather?" asked Louis with a touch of his old humour.

"We could swap," suggested well-mannered Jim.

"Thank you very much!" said the young hunter.

"Why not?" asked Jim.

"Your jacket would not fit me," said Louis.

"We could try, though," replied the practical Jim, already trying to relieve "Sir" of his jacket. But "Sir" did not seem to be in such a hurry.

"Just a moment," he said; "I'll just take my revolver out first. It would be a pity to lose my gun — it is brand new!"

At this piece of information, Bob and Jim looked at each other, startled. Jim was of the opinion that it was high time for Bob to knock this imperturbable traveller over the head with his awe-inspiring cudgel. But Bob did not seem to be very confident, and Jim realized that he would have to do it himself. He gripped his heavy cudgel firmly in his strong hand, but the amazing stranger said evenly, "Drop that club, man, or I will have to use my revolver!"

"Bob!" urged Jim. "Bob!"

"Bob isn't going to do anything," said the stranger. "Bob, give up your club!"

There seemed to be some magic power in this stranger, for Bob automatically gave up the cudgel.

"Think of my poor wife and children!" he pleaded.

"Have you gone totally crazy?" said Jim through clenched teeth. "You blockhead!" and he raised his arm for the blow.

But young Wessels avoided the cudgel by quickly leaping aside, and sent the thief sprawling to the ground with one blow of his fist.

When Jim tried to get up, Louis said, "Lie down, man, lie down!"

So Jim remained on the ground, seeing the revolver and hearing it being cocked.

An extraordinary idea came to Louis. He was in a mood in which he craved diversion, a dangerous exploit. Turning to Bob, he said: "Where do you live, Bob?"

"Half an hour from here — in the *veld*."

"Are you married?"

"I have a wife who is ill and six children who are starving, Sir!"

"I want to investigate this — come along!"

Bob was frightened by this proposal and he threw the stranger a quick, suspicious glance, while Jim used the opportunity to escape into the shrubs. Bob suspected that he was dealing with an undercover policeman, and his heart began to beat faster. He looked to the left and right for a thornbush in which to hide, but the young hunter said, "Don't try any dumb tricks, Bob — do you know how many cartridges I have in my revolver?"

"Six cartridges, Sir!"

"There are fifteen, Bob!"

"Fifteen cartridges!" said Bob in a trembling voice, shuddering.

"Yes, fifteen, my dear fellow," said Louis. "So, walk a little faster!"

In this way they reached Bob's home — an old wooden hut with sod walls.

"You first," commanded the young Boer, and Bob pushed the unlocked door open.

It was pitch-dark inside.

"Make a fire so we can have some light and warmth!" Louis ordered.

Bob obeyed automatically, gathering some wood which he laid on the fire in the fireplace. Then he felt for the table to find matches, but Wessels had anticipated him.

"Here's a match," he said, striking a match and handing it to Bob. The fire in the hearth soon flared up brilliantly, lighting a neat but very poor interior.

Bob looked stealthily at the stranger. He had seen him before, but where had it been? Ah, now he knew. It had been the previous year when he had to convey twenty large baskets of apricots to Ladysmith for Master Arend Uys.

From a bed in the corner a plaintive voice called, "Bob, husband — are you back?"

He hurried to the bed. "Here I am," he said kindly.

"This is not a highwayman's family," thought the young hunter, staring ahead of him into the fire.

"Have you caught anything, dear?"

"Game is becoming scarce, wife — I haven't caught anything."

"Then he *is* a highwayman," thought Louis, and the thought hurt him.

"Who is there with you? Not Jim, I hope?"

Bob shook his head.

"Are you waiting for Jim? He leads you astray in dangerous wicked ways. I don't like the looks of him. He is capable of murder and robbery."

There was a moment of silence.

The face of the young Boer had lit up again, for in the last words he had realized his own mistake. He sat down on a wooden stool, and Pluto shook the water from his shaggy wet coat.

"Who is with you?" asked the sick housewife in a low voice.

Bob shrugged. "I don't know," he answered in the same tone.

"What does he want here in the middle of the night?"

"He came in to warm himself," said Bob. "He is soaked to the skin by the rain."

"I had hoped that you would catch something," complained the sick woman, "then we would have had some meat to give our poor children in the morning."

"Where are your children?" asked the stranger all of a sudden.

"There!" said Bob, pointing to the opposite corner of the room.

Yes, there they were — on the ground, huddled under a heap of sacks and old clothes. In the flickering light of the fire the Boer could make out the pale faces of the children, who were sleeping peacefully.

Their poverty cut into his soul.

"Bob," he said warmly, "come and sit with me by the fire, and tell me where you come from."

"I was born in England, Sir," said Bob. "I worked on the gold mines of the Witwatersrand, became sick there, and this is where I ended up."

Wessels had been afraid that Bob belonged to the Rednecks, and he was sorry about that, but what could be done about it? Could Bob help it?

"I am cold. Make me a cup of coffee, Bobby!"

"I only have enough for one cup, Sir — for my wife for tomorrow morning, and then it will be finished."

It did Louis good to see that Bob felt so much for his sick wife, and he faced him with a friendly look. But the wife called from the poorly-covered bed, "Give it to the poor stranger, husband, for he must be soaked by the rain, and it will refresh him!"

"You have a good wife, Bob," said Louis, while Bob was preparing to make the coffee.

"Sir, she is everything to me," said Bob in a low voice, fearing that Louis would make known his exploits. Of course this was due to the things he had on his conscience. A guilty conscience makes one very uneasy.

The coffee had now been made and from a wooden cupboard Bob took an old-fashioned cup with faded gold lettering.

"Get another one!" said Louis.

"For whom?" asked Bob.

"For whom? For you, of course, Bob."

"There won't be enough, Sir."

"There *must* be enough, Bob — we'll share and share alike."

So Bob took another cup from the wooden cupboard. It was cracked, but looked clean, just like the first one. As a matter of fact, in spite of the extreme poverty, the whole room spoke of discipline, cleanliness, and order.

Louis studied the cup in the glow of the fire. It read: "Out of love."

"That is a nice motto, Bob."

"It is about the only one remaining of the cups we got when we were married."

"Do you ever quarrel now that you are married, Bob?"

"Quarrel, Sir? We toil from morning until evening to have bread for the hungry mouths of our children, and my wife does everything possible to make my burden lighter — when would we have the time to quarrel? It's a luxury we can't afford."

"Poor people have privileges," said the young Boer. "They are protected from a lot of misery."

Bob gave young Wessels a surprised look at these words, and for a moment he thought the stranger was not all there. However, he didn't look like a lunatic, so Bob dismissed the thought.

He took the brass coffee pot now and poured some for Louis, who drank the hot coffee. The brown liquid was good for him; he was beginning to get warm while the fire in the hearth made steam rise from his wet clothes.

Then he got up and put a gold coin into Bob's hand. It gleamed in the light of the fire.

"A sovereign!" exclaimed Bob in joyful surprise. "A sovereign!"

He turned the coin over and over, but then it suddenly seemed like it was starting to glow and burn in his hand, so he put it down on the rough table.

"Put it in your pocket, Bob!"

"Oh Sir," said Bob, "it is too much for me!"

He went outside and Louis followed him, for he knew the struggle in the man's heart.

"Sir," said Bob when they came outside, "tonight was the first time that I went out to rob someone. You may not believe me, but God knows it's the truth. I could no longer bear the poverty in my home. And the man I attacked now gives me a sovereign of his own free will — that cuts me to the quick! It's too much for me! It's too much for me!"

"Never mind," said the young Boer. "I have forgiven you already, Bob! Let's go inside again, otherwise your wife will be worried."

So they entered the house again.

"What happened?" asked the sick wife in a bewildered state.

"Wife," Bob cried, pure joy beaming from his face, "this man gave us a sovereign — a real gold sovereign!"

"A sovereign," she repeated. "A sovereign! Now we can buy bread for our children, and some clothes, and meat — Oh Bob, we are richer than kings! I thought he was a poor stranger, but he is an envoy from our heavenly Father who always rescues us when our need is greatest."

She folded her thin hands and whispered, "Praise the LORD, O my soul, and forget not all His benefits!"

Louis was now ready to leave, but the sick woman asked: "Have you thanked our benefactor, husband?"

"I will show him the way to the railway station," answered Bob, "and then buy what we need in the town."

"You stay here," answered the young hunter. "Pluto and I will be able to find the way!"

But Bob was determined to go along. Also, he was afraid that Jim might risk attacking once more.

The storm had subsided, and the rain had stopped, but a strong wind was still blowing. The first streaks of dawn could be seen by the time Wessels and his new acquaintance reached the railway station.

Chapter VIII
In the Train

Bob had taken leave of young Wessels, and sitting down on the hard bench in the waiting-room, Louis began reflecting on the extraordinary adventure he had had in the past night.

There was reason to hope that Bob wouldn't return to the occupation he had practised for the first time the previous night, but with Jim it was a different matter. He would probably remain a highwayman unless something out of the ordinary intervened. The previous night was not the first time he had tried to make a catch. Having himself been led astray earlier, he had now led Bob astray. So there was little hope for him; one day he would be arrested and would be unable to escape ten or twenty years in solitary confinement and hard labour. Of course — it would be what he deserved, there was nothing wrong with that. Thieves go to prison, and murderers to the gallows.

But what punishment was there for those who thieved and murdered on a larger scale, who in their insatiable thirst for gold would not hesitate to wipe out an entire nation?

"They're just Jingoists," muttered the young Boer through clenched teeth. "Oh, those Jingoists!"

The old wound was ripped open once more with renewed pain. But he did not regret having broken off with Truida Uys, for he could never bend his strong, free neck under the British yoke — he would much rather die!

The approaching train broke into these thoughts. He secured a humble seat in the corner of a full compartment.

The train was almost ready to depart. The thin railway clerk nudged the stationmaster, saying, "Have you seen the Transvaal Boer? Sent home with a flea in his ear — I am sure of it!" He clutched at his own neck, which seemed even thinner and scrawnier than the day before.

But the stationmaster did not have time to listen to the chatter of his subordinate. He gave the signal for departure, the bell rang, the steam whistle answered, and the train began to move forward.

Louis Wessels stared sadly out the window at the hilly countryside stretching along the railway tracks while the conversation of his fellow-passengers hummed about his ears.

Next to him sat a heavily-built woman with a basket full of knick-knacks she was going to sell. Her four-year-old daughter was sitting next to her. The pale woman sitting opposite the vendor-woman proved to be a midwife, swamping the vendor-woman with a wealth of old wives' tales. But the broad-shouldered vendor-woman was not about to accept everything she was told, and it became a serious dispute when the midwife stood her ground on the opinion that a corn on the left foot was a better barometer than one on the right foot.

Referees were called in to settle the important question, but a sailor on the next seat spat on the floor and said contemptuously, "What boring chatter!" Whereupon the women suspended their discussion for a while.

But then the little girl thought it was a good time to say something. She pulled on her mother's sleeve and, pointing to a huge bird which was going up the hill with long slow steps, asked, "What kind of bird is that, Mummy?"

"An ostrich," said the vendor-woman, who was rearranging her wares.

"Why doesn't he fly, Mummy?"

"His wings are too short to fly, Child!"

"Then what does an ostrich do, Mummy?"

"He is always looking for naughty children."

"But I'm not naughty, Mummy, am I?"

"No, you're a sweet child, but don't make my head spin with all these questions."

"Does an ostrich also have children, Mummy?"

"Of course."

"Does the stork bring those children too, Mummy?"

"No," said the mother, who was beginning to lose her temper. "A hippo does."

"What does a hippo do, Mummy?"

"It wades through the water!" said the mother, doing her best not to sound unkind.

"Then does he take a bath?"

"Yes, he takes a bath."

"Is he very fat?"

"Yes, he is very fat."

"How fat, Mummy?"

"As thick as a tower and if you don't shut up, I'll give you a box on the ear."

Naturally the little one began howling, so that the midwife got in her stab by saying, "I suppose you do not have much experience with children?"

Whereupon the vendor answered in a high-pitched voice, "I have brought up thirteen of them to be good and honest people — goodbye, everyone! Come on, Betty, come Dear, this is our station. — And fortunately not one of them is too free in their speech, Mistress Midwife! Goodbye!"

The compartment had a little more room now, but to his chagrin, Louis Wessels saw the unavoidable British uniform. A corporal, already on in years, and three young recruits were entering. All four were in infantry uniform. They seated themselves next to the young hunter.

Nothing could be said about their attitude. They behaved calmly and with dignity and had friendly, kind faces. One of the recruits took a letter from his shirt pocket, the second started to read a New Testament attentively, while the corporal and the third recruit sat talking about the probability of war in a tone that could not hurt young Wessels in any way.

Of course they took the English point of view and lamented the unyielding stubbornness of the Boers, but for the rest they spoke more in a strain of concern and sympathy than of hate and passion.

"But they haven't subdued the Boers yet!" Louis chipped in.

"Are you a Transvaal Boer?" asked the corporal.

"I am," said Louis.

"If you have influence with your government, advise them to be accommodating, for our government won't yield any farther."

"Neither will the Transvaal government," said Louis.

"Those poor Boers!" said the corporal. "They will spill their own blood and gain nothing!"

"We have God and justice on our side," said Louis calmly.

"So you claim," said the corporal, "but we also claim that."

"We will overcome our enemies," said Louis.

"Yes, that's what you think, but you have no idea of England's power! If you take a thousand Englishmen prisoner, ten thousand will come in their place. If you shoot down five thousand Englishmen, fifty thousand will take up their posts."

"If God gives us the strength to overcome the elite troops of the British, we have finished the job. The rest does not amount to much."

"You do not know the power of Britain," said the corporal somewhat heatedly. "She will simply crush your commandos by the overwhelming numbers of her troops."

"We are not afraid of eighty thousand British troops."

"Well, then England will send two or three times that number."

The young Boer shrugged.

"I don't know where England will get them."

"You will find that out to your own distress, man. England has a huge purse and unlimited credit."

"Of course England will scrape together a number of men," mocked Louis. "All of them mercenaries, who are paid per shift to be brave."

But Louis was sorry that he had spoken of mercenaries. The corporal seemed to have taken offence, and did not want to continue the conversation. He was altogether silent.

At that moment a blast of wind blew off the cap of the recruit sitting opposite the young Boer, and in his haste to catch it, he would have gone through the door which was not properly closed. Louis prevented him from being hurled out of the speeding train by grabbing him around the waist.

The whole incident didn't take more than a few seconds, and passed unnoticed by most of the passengers. But the soldier who had been rescued wanted to show his gratitude, so he offered the young Boer his last cigar. Louis refused since it was his last, only taking it when he realized that it would please the recruit.

But he did not light it. His heart which was still deeply wounded by the events of only the day before, was full of sorrow, and sadly he gazed through the window.

"Do light up," said the young soldier, lighting the third match, "I think you had a greater fright than I did."

Then the young hunter did light the cigar.

"Do you know what I was just thinking?" he said, and his voice became warm and friendly. "I was thinking that if we should meet one another on the battlefield we would kill one another like brutes! Isn't that absolutely terrible? Wouldn't it be better for the criminal who has this terrible war on his conscience to have a millstone bound around his neck and be thrown into the deep sea?"

The young soldier nodded that he agreed.

"The real question is who that criminal is," he said.

"That question has been answered already," said Louis.

"By whom?"

"By the collective conscience of all nations in the world," said Louis emphatically.

The soldier who had been reading from the New Testament now closed his little Bible.

"It may be that justice is on the side of the Boers," he said earnestly. "I can't be sure."

"And you still dare fight against us with such a possibility?" asked young Wessels, hurt and amazed.

"I owe blind obedience to my officers," answered the soldier. "I have sworn to be faithful to the flag, and I may not commit perjury."

Wessels wanted to answer to this, but then he thought better of it — what would be the use?

They had now reached the next station. The train stopped, and the four soldiers got out. They shook hands with the young Boer, who reciprocated with sincerity.

Tomorrow or the next day they would stand against one another as sworn enemies! And if the Boer did not get the chance to put a bullet through their heads, he had the chance of being stabbed by a razor-sharp bayonet.

The young hunter shuddered as though he had a fever, and sat gazing silently out upon the hilly countryside, which stretched out peacefully before his eyes.

Chapter IX
Two Standpoints

Aunt Sannie was looking through the small window of the cookhouse, situated near the house, when she saw Louis approaching on his bay. She immediately realized that something serious must have occurred.

Louis sat down beside her in the little cookhouse, laying his arm on the broad window-sill and recounted the sad end to his engagement. The young man found comfort in baring his wounded soul to her loving mother-heart while no one else had yet heard about it.

Mother Wessels listened attentively, now and then shaking her head, looking calm and wise but saying nothing. When he had finished speaking, a quiet smile played around her lips, and she said, "You have both behaved like a pair of silly children."

"Mother," Louis said in utter amazement, "I couldn't do *anything* else."

"You are a pair of dim-witted, silly children," said Aunt Sannie calmly, "and I believe that you are the sillier of the two. But do go in now — John is there, John Walker!"

John was one of Louis' best friends, who as a child had spent a number of years in the hospitable home of *Wonderfontein* as one the family. John's parents had been English. They had died in poverty. On the deathbed of John's mother, an outspoken Christian, the Afrikaans Samaritan had promised that he would take care of her child. The promise had eased her passing, and Gijs Wessels had kept his promise. So young John had arrived as a small child at *Wonderfontein* where he was disciplined when necessary, and where he developed very well.

A friendly child by nature, he felt attached to his foster-parents for whom he felt reverence and gratitude, and showed in his behaviour that he was fond of them. There was no obvious difference between him and a Transvaaler. He was an excellent marksman, although not as good as Louis — but then, who could compete in shooting with the young hunter? — and was accepted by the Boers.

But it was still a pity that he was not an Afrikaner by birth, and although he had more than once said to old Wessels, "Your God is my God," the other words that Wessels would have liked to hear: "Your people are my people!" never passed his lips.

The mysterious voice of his blood drove him to side with England, and as he grew older, that voice became louder. Maybe that was why, when he was old enough to earn his own living, he had not wanted to stay in Transvaal but had sought a job in Natal. This he had easily found because he was intelligent and quick to learn. But the ties which bound him to *Wonderfontein* were not severed because of this. They never would be, and John had shed secret tears because his foster-parents were saddened by his siding with the English.

Every year John Walker spent several days at *Wonderfontein* as an always-welcome guest. It had always been his silent hope that the English and the Afrikaners would be able to meet as sincere friends. But it didn't seem as though his hope would be fulfilled. When heavy clouds had gathered in the political sky of South Africa four years earlier, Jameson's raid had been like a bolt of lightning in a dark night.

In the meantime old Wessels was comforted by the fact that in the matter of the *uitlanders* John stood firmly on the side of the Boers, and that he called Chamberlain's Jingoistic policy impious and despicable.

Yet he did not agree with Louis in his hope that in response to England's fearsome military preparations the Transvaal government would proclaim war on England and occupy northern Natal. He could see no justification for such conduct; as a matter of fact, he condemned the idea and said outright that he would join the British troops as a volunteer if the colony of Natal was occupied by the Boers.

Yet it would not go that far. The tension had been relieved again. The threatening war would be averted. John had heard it in Pretoria, and although he had made a considerable detour to visit *Wonderfontein* it did not prevent him from surprising his old friends with the latest news. The news was that Paul Kruger had consented to England's original demand of the "five-year franchise" on condition that England would drop its claim to suzerainty altogether, and would in the future have all differences with the Boers settled by an arbiter. John felt sure that the greatest danger of war had now disappeared, and Gijs Wessels was overjoyed by the news.

"You are an Ahimaaz — a bearer of good tidings!" he said cheerfully, filling a fresh pipe.

At this moment Louis entered the living-room and the two friends greeted each other most heartily.

They were about the same age, both strong and well-built, flourishing in the strength of their youth. But their moods differed greatly at that moment. Even the good news brought by John could not lift the dejected spirits of the young hunter.

"It's no use," he said, "none whatsoever! Chamberlain will reject Kruger's proposals and the war will be inevitable."

"There's still the Liberal Party in England," said John. "They will not approve of an unjust war."

"The English Liberal Party!" Louis scoffed. "They are rundown — they belong in a nursing home!"

Mother Wessels entered with her guest, the sick teacher. He held onto her arm. Louis was shocked to see that in a few days the condition of the sick man had deteriorated considerably.

"How are you?" he asked sympathetically.

"I'm well," said the sick man; "quite well!" and he sank down into an armchair which Aunt Sannie had placed for him with motherly care.

Louis shook his head.

"Don't you understand?" said the consumptive man. "The journey is getting short. Soon I'll be home."

"Are you not afraid of the valley of the shadow of death?" Louis asked.

"The valley is lit up by the red of the dawn of the resurrection. To be released and to be with Christ — it is by far the best!"

He had a sudden fit of coughing and his body shook like a dilapidated house when a storm rages around it.

"Mother Wessels," he said after a while, "I am cold — I would like to go to bed."

So Aunt Sannie helped him up and brought him to his bed in the small guest room.

The patient lived five more days. Then he quietly breathed his last. Mother Wessels, Louis, and Daniel were present when he died.

"Are you not at all afraid of dying, William?" asked Daniel.

"No, my boy," said the dying man, "I have been tempted sorely in the last few days by the Evil One, but now I know for sure that my sins have been forgiven. Jesus is my Saviour."

"And you are glad to die?"

"Yes, Daniel."

"Why, William?"

"I'm now reaching my goal, to serve God eternally without sin."

He closed his eyes to pray; he folded his trembling hands one last time.

"Pray also for the poor Afrikaner people!" whispered Daniel.

The sick man's eyes opened wide.

"The man is dying, Daniel," said Louis with a soft reproach in his voice. Yet the lamp of his life flared up once more, and while Daniel supported his hands raised in prayer, the dying man pleaded with his God in an startlingly clear voice for the plight of the Afrikaans people.

Suddenly his voice broke off, and his hands fell heavily into Daniel's hands.

"He has passed away," said Mother Wessels sorrowfully.

Daniel, who was bending over him, shook his head. He had once more felt the breath of the dying man.

And indeed his mouth was still moving; it seemed as though a Psalm was lingering on his dying lips — but the sound died away gradually like the sound of a dying summer breeze in the tops of the trees . . .

They were all deeply moved, as the evening sun caressed the marble-white features.

"Shouldn't we take his hands apart?" asked Mother Wessels.

"Leave him as he is, Mother," said Daniel; "he died with his hands folded, praying for our people — let him rest with folded hands in his last home!"

So he was buried like that, the folded hands resting on the white shroud.

Chapter X
Leaving Home

The young hunter had been right: England wanted war, and his father, old Wessels, was very troubled. He had prayed long and sincerely that this trial might be kept from his people.

The master of *Wonderfontein* would go to war with a heavy heart. He was a husband and a father, and saw the war in a different light than Kees and Karel, whose young and untroubled hearts went into the war as though it were a hunting party.

Still, he did not hesitate to go to war for those reasons.

How could he possibly have hesitated! The ghosts of his ancestors would have risen from their graves to regard him with angry gestures if he would dare to renounce the traditions of his people. The walls of the state of Transvaal had risen slowly, and its bricks had been laid in a strong and solid mortar of blood and tears. And the Wessels family had contributed a considerable part of this mortar, for they were of the small but tough band of Gideon which formed the real salt and the pith of the Afrikaans nation, as God willed it.

No, there was not a shadow of hesitation on the part of Gijs Wessels, and if at times the thought of war brought fear to his heart, it was fear more for his people than for himself. For he bore this people in his heart, and he would gladly have given his own blood if by doing so he could ensure the independence and vigour, and especially the spiritual vigour, of his beloved people.

Aunt Sannie had all the time nurtured the hope that the Lord would prevent the war with a miracle. It was only when an officer rode into the yard and delivered the document calling upon Gijs Wessels and his three elder sons to appear in full military dress in two days' time at the commando's meeting place, that her hope died like a lamp which had used its last drop of oil.

Gijs Wessels received the document personally. His sons were out in the *veld*, for it was lambing season. Toward evening they

The Recruiting Officer

came home. On the way they had already heard about the government's mobilization order from some blacks.

On hearing the news Kees and Karel threw their hats into the air and shouted, "Hurrah! We'll shoot the Redcoats like wild pigeons!"

This news brought relief to Louis. True, during the last two weeks he had lost the overconfidence Kees and Karel still displayed in the school of suffering, but the command to mobilize was a relief after the endless uncertainty. He was convinced that the little ship had to go through the dangers of the storm before it could ride at anchor in the safety of the harbour. Conscious of his own young strength, he now felt that war was inevitable — the sooner it began, the better. About Truida Uys he no longer spoke; such was his tough nature. But Aunt Sannie knew well in her heart that no one, not even Paul Kruger, had made a greater sacrifice for the interest of their people than had her son Louis.

All day long Mother Wessels and Janske had been busy baking rusks, preparing *biltong*, and seeing to the uniforms of the Boers who would be setting out in the morning. Busy the whole day taking care of all the preparations for the coming campaign, they had not had much time to speak. But now everything was done, and the family sat down together for the evening meal, earlier than usual.

Yet even at this meal little was said. An oppressive atmosphere seemed to weigh on the family.

"You will have to take my place on the farm in my absence," said Gijs Wessels, giving his youngest son a pat on the shoulder.

"Must I stay at home then, Father?" Daniel asked in a surprised voice.

The master of *Wonderfontein* was no less surprised than his son. Daniel had often declared that he would have nothing to do with a war, and now he was volunteering to go along. Gijs Wessels did not understand that; Daniel seemed to have changed his mind suddenly.

"Of course you must stay at home," said Gijs Wessels; "it stands to reason."

"Let me go along!" pleaded Daniel.

"You are much too young," said his father.

"Then I am also too young to take your place," returned Daniel.

For the first time in his life he had challenged a decision made by his father.

"I suppose you have made him enthusiastic for the war," said Master Wessels, turning to Kees and Karel, but both could truthfully say that Daniel was speaking of his own accord.

"Please stay here!" said Mother Wessels, attached as she was to Daniel, her Benjamin.

"Of course he will stay here," said Father Wessels in a tone of voice which would tolerate no opposition, and Daniel was silent. Not a word more did he utter, looking out through sad eyes.

The meal was concluded in silence, and the family went to bed earlier than usual, for they were to depart early in the morning.

Master Wessels could not sleep, and when at last he fell asleep, he had a strange and unique dream.

He was standing on top of a hill, below which was a dry riverbed. An Afrikaans Boer approached with a bandoleer across his chest. From a gaping wound in his chest spurted warm red blood, staining the dry riverbed. Then came another Boer, then many more — graybeards, men, and youths — and their blood filled the dry riverbed. And among the Boers moved groups of widows and orphans in long black mourning garments, and they sat weeping by that River of Blood, and their tears swelled the river to a great and dreadful stream.

And Master Wessels became very sorrowful on seeing this.

But slowly, very slowly, the long, sad procession of graybeards, men, and youths, and of widows and orphans, who had fed that terrible river with their blood and tears came to an end. The river subsided within its banks and the stream of blood dried up. And from the riverbed a temple arose — a great and glorious temple, and above its golden gates was written in letters flashing like gems: "Blessed is the people whose God is the LORD!"

He saw his Afrikaans brothers going up to this house of prayer, but no longer did they wear bandoleers across their chests, or have bleeding wounds. He also saw the women going up, but they no longer had tears in their eyes, and the children going up were clad in festive garments. All the bells began to peal, and from the house of prayer rose a Psalm to the glory of God:

> *Come and be to my words attentive,*
> *All you who the Almighty fear.*
> *Let me declare how He has helped me,*
> *How in my troubles He drew near.*
> *I cried to God in my affliction,*
> *And He in mercy heard my voice;*
> *I sang His praise with exultation.*
> *In His compassion I rejoice.*[*]

---

[*] Psalm 66:7, *Book of Praise: Anglo-Genevan Psalter.*

Suddenly he woke up. It seemed that he could still hear the notes of the Psalm. He sat up, and in the starlight which came in through the unshuttered windows, looked around the room.

Halfway between the bed and the window stood Daniel.

"Were *you* singing, Daniel?" his father asked.

"A Boers commando is passing by," said Daniel. "Listen, you can still hear them singing."

"All right, my boy, now go to bed!" said his father.

"Let me go along with you, Father," pleaded the boy. "Let me fight with you!"

"Would you leave your mother alone?" asked Gijs Wessels.

"Can I leave *you* alone?" replied Daniel. "In the dangers of the war?"

"You are still a child and you will become afraid when the enemies' bullets whistle through the air."

Daniel shook his head.

"I will pray the Lord to give me a brave heart, Father!"

"And if you should fall in battle, Daniel?"

"Then I would have given my young life for the freedom of my people."

"That would be terrible, Daniel!"

"No indeed, Father — it would be a glorious death, the death of a hero for freedom and justice. Not many are chosen for that."

He said these words with great emphasis, and there was an unusual light in his soft eyes.

"Do you know where you will go when you die, Daniel?"

"To the heavenly home of my Father."

"You speak with great certainty — you are only a child, Daniel."

"Does that prevent the Holy Spirit from assuring me that the Lord Jesus has bought me with his precious blood?"

"No, my son, it certainly is no obstacle," Master Wessels said with conviction.

From the adjoining room came the deep, regular breathing of the other sons.

"Go to bed now, my son," said Master Wessels. "It is still night."

"May I go along then, Father?" the boy pleaded once more. He took hold of his father's hands, and Master Wessels felt his warm tears falling on them. They overcame his resistance.

Daniel was allowed to go along.

The first rays of morning light could be seen. The stable doors were wide open. About ten sleepy black men were bringing the horses out and saddled them.

In the living room Gijs Wessels was sitting with his family for the last breakfast. He went outside and saw the four bridled horses. "Get Daniel's pony ready too!" he ordered and returned to the house.

Little was said, even less than the night before. Even Kees and Karel were feeling dejected. All hearts were full. Daniel was sitting next to his mother. He could not swallow his bread, and he was holding her hands as if never to let go again.

The rooster courageously crowed a loud greeting to the morning. The horses stood neighing and stamping their feet in front of the house.

Breakfast was done, and Master Wessels read in a deeply moved voice from Psalm one hundred and thirty:

> *A Song of degrees.*
> *Out of the depths have I cried unto Thee, O LORD.*
> *Lord, hear my voice: let Thine ears be attentive to the voice of my supplications.*
> *If Thou, LORD, shouldest mark iniquities, O Lord, who shall stand?*
> *But there is forgiveness with Thee, that Thou mayest be feared.*
> *I wait for the LORD, my soul doth wait, and in His word do I hope.*
> *My soul waiteth for the Lord more than they that watch for the morning: I say, more than they that watch for the morning.*
> *Let Israel hope in the LORD: for with the LORD there is mercy, and with Him is plenteous redemption.*
> *And He shall redeem Israel from all his iniquities.*

Then they knelt down and Gijs Wessels lifted up his hands to call down the blessing of the Almighty on his family and his people.

In the corner stood the rifles. Mother Wessels herself hung the bandoleer filled with bullets on the broad chest of the master of *Wonderfontein*.

Then they went outside. The couple tarried some moments under the spreading old lime tree.

"Do you remember, Sannie, how we pledged our love under this tree?"

The spring breeze quieted down and whispered softly over the new green leaves of the old tree. He held her right hand in both of his, her left hand resting on his shoulder.

"Do you remember it, Sannie?"

How well she remembered it!

Daniel pressed against his mother, but Janske took his hat and stuck a large black feather in it.

Kees and Karel could feel tears welling in their eyes, but Louis had already mounted his horse. Sitting there on his tall bay, his hawk-eyes exploring the horizon, he really was the hunter, the young hunter, the great hunter. Only this time he was not going to hunt the nimble deer on the mountain, but the Redneck who was seeking to hem in his people.

White mist was rising from the valleys, but the rising sun was already burning it off, covering the rich young spring life in a golden glow.

The Boers mounted quickly. One more silent press of the hand — the spirited horses felt the spurs — and they took the lane at a gallop.

Mother Wessels and Janske gazed after them with sorrow in their hearts — how painful it was to part!

The horsemen had reached the hill, and Daniel looked back one last time. He gave the very last farewell, waving with his Mauser. Then he disappeared from his mother's eye behind the hill. For a moment she could still see the barrel of the gun, shining in the morning sun — and then alas, they were gone — gone!

Chapter XI
Around the Campfires

There was a great hustle and bustle near the Buffalo River in Natal territory. Horses were being watered, oxen were put out to graze, tents were being pitched, and a camp was being formed in a large square with hundreds of wagons.

A few days before, on October 11, 1899, war had actually broken out, when the Transvaal government had sent an ultimatum. They *had* to do this, they were forced to. Looking on passively while England was making massive preparations to destroy the Republic would have been equal to tempting God and committing suicide.

Evening was drawing near, and at one of the hundreds of brightly-burning campfires a group of burghers was gathered, among whom were Louis with his two brothers, Kees and Karel, Blijvenstein and his former servant, Blikoortje.

It would seem a strange coincidence that brought these two, Blijvenstein and Blikoortje, together at one campfire, but actually it was not strange, for this war had called up every able-bodied man of the two Boer republics to take up arms.

Kees and Karel were lying at full length by the fire, their chins supported in their sturdy hands, while on their handsome faces youthful mischief could be read. Their young hearts had long since gotten over the sadness of the parting at *Wonderfontein*, and the beginning of the campaign with its adventures and ups and downs looked most attractive in their carefree view.

Louis was carefully examining his brand-new Mauser in the firelight, hoping in the course of this campaign to retain the name he had as the best marksman in the commando.

Blijvenstein had sat down on a stone near the fire, and was busy repairing the shabby saddle of his long-legged horse while Blikoortje impertinently squatted on his haunches next to his former master.

"Come on, Blikoortje," said Karel, "gather some more wood, my man, and poke up the fire!"

The young Free Stater complied with this request and now stood in the full light of the flaring flames.

"You look as if you haven't washed for four weeks, man!" Karel gave his opinion as he looked at the young servant's tanned face.

"You should really clean up a bit before going into battle with the Redcoats!" advised Kees in a friendly tone.

"The bravest heroes were always the dirtiest fellows," Blikoortje laughed. "The old Sea Beggars in the Eighty Years' War thought they were particularly clean if they washed once in two years."

"Where was the last place you worked?" asked Karel, poking the fire with a long stick.

"I worked for a mistress who was cross-eyed and always spied on me. She had three big canine teeth with which she ground her food. I had just decided to pack up and go when I was called up."

"You never stay long in one place," said Blijvenstein. "Shall I tell you what your biggest fault is?"

"That *I* eat the roasted chickens and leave the cats for *you*!" joked Blikoortje in good spirits, causing the young Boers to burst into loud roars of laughter.

But that made Blijvenstein angry, and he shot back with a resentful look, "You are too cheeky, little squirt; that is your fault. Your mouth is too big."

With an awl he pierced a hole in the saddle and tried to thread the wire through it.

"I went hungry in your service, that's for sure!" replied Blikoortje.

Blijvenstein now succeeded in threading the wire through the opening.

"You see, friends, it is just as I told you," he said, "the boy is very rude."

"You better look out that the Redcoats don't get hold of you," joked Blikoortje.

"One could wish that everybody felt as deeply for our just cause as I do!" Blijvenstein said emphatically.

"There is much chaff among the grain," he resumed, making a covert reference to the young servant, while he hammered at the shabby old saddle.

"There are cowards galore," said the young hunter, looking up from his rifle for a moment, "maybe even among us."

" 'Much chaff among the grain,' " joked Blikoortje, repeating Blijvenstein's words, "and Master Blijvenstein belongs to the grain, but . . . now I'm lying."

"You are a wicked brat," grumbled Master Blijvenstein.

"Pardon me, Master?"

"That you are a wicked brat!"

"I don't understand you, Master!"

But Master Blijvenstein was wise enough to keep quiet. He threw aside the hammer and took up the awl again.

"I suppose you did good business with that English horse-dealer, Master?"

"I know nothing about an English horse-dealer, you rascal."

"The one to whom you sold six salted mares* at a scandalously high price, Master."

"Was that an Englishman?" Blijvenstein asked, shrugging his shoulders. "Goodness, I had no idea!"

"Of course you had no idea. You probably thought they were intended for our government artillery, and not for the English cavalry."

"I have nothing to do with your gossip, you impudent lout," said Blijvenstein, getting up to look closely at the repaired saddle by the light of the fire.

"Is that true?" asked Kees Wessels with contempt in his voice. "Did he really sell horses intended for the English horsemen?"

"Well, he says he knows nothing about it," said Blikoortje.

Master Blijvenstein did not seem to enjoy their company, and went away to another campfire. The young Boers were only too glad, and drew a little closer to the cosy fire while Blikoortje regaled them with an endless store of funny stories.

---

* Salted mares were ones that had had the African horse sickness and were therefore immune to it. Thus they were quite valuable.

Now it was long evening. The campfires of the Boers stretched for miles like a flaming chain of light. The Pleiades could be seen twinkling in the sky, and the Almighty Creator wrote His glory in the tens of thousands of shining and twinkling diamonds of the Milky Way, which stretched in silent majesty above the camp of the Boers.

Then from the far end of the camp the stately notes of a Psalm could be heard. The melody swelled like a stream overflowing its banks. Rising from their campfire, the young Boers took off their hats, and their fresh young voices united with thousands of others in the war Psalm of the Boers:

God shall arise and by His might
Put all His enemies to flight;
In conquest shall He quell them.
Let those who hate Him, scattered, flee
Before His glorious majesty,
For God Himself shall fell them.
Just as the wind drives smoke away,
So God will scatter the array
Of those who evil cherish.
As wax that melts before the fire,
So, vanquished by God's dreadful ire,
Shall all the wicked perish.[*]

When the last notes of the Psalm died away on the hills of Natal and along the banks of the Buffalo River all was quiet again. The Boers wrapped themselves in their blankets and lay down under the ox wagons, in the tents, or under the starry sky.

Everything became very peaceful. The neighing of the horses subsided, the oxen lay down drowsily, and only the wing-beat of a night bird could be heard high in the sky.

_____

[*] Psalm 68:1, *Book of Praise*: *Anglo-Genevan Psalter*.

Chapter XII
Going to War

There was a rumour that the commandos from Pretoria, Vryheid, and Utrecht would march on Dundee immediately with the aim of ousting or cutting off General Symons who was entrenched there, while the army under General Jan Kock, which included the Wessels family, would keep to the right with the aim of breaking up the railway line between Ladysmith and Glencoe, and taking up a strong position in the passes of the Waschbank mountain.

Karel and Kees were very eager for a speedy encounter with the enemy, and asked permission of their father to join one of the commandos marching on Dundee, in which were also a number of relatives and acquaintances of the Wessels family. After hesitating initially, he gave them permission, and when the officer making the decisions on this also consented, Kees and Karel joined the Vryheid commando to Dundee.

The army of General Jan Kock, among whose members were also Gijs Wessels with his two sons, Louis and Daniel, departed in the middle of the night to Elandslaagte. It was a cold night, and an icy wind was sweeping over the mountains. Daniel rode next to his father. He was wrapped in a long raincoat, and shivering with cold. When they were about halfway, the march was forced to a halt by an ammunition wagon with a broken wheel, and only when this had been repaired could they proceed.

At dawn they halted, and the commander gave the order to unsaddle. The horses were hobbled and guards posted, and the tired horsemen lay down on the ground, wrapped in their blankets.

Daniel was soon fast asleep, but old Wessels felt no desire to follow suit, so he sat down on a rock near his son. At that moment he regretted having brought along the boy, for Daniel was not strong, and his pale features were already marked by the unaccustomed fatigue of the campaign. He had put a saddle under his head, but his solicitous father thought that too hard a pillow; he took off his overcoat, rolled it up, and pushed it under the boy's head in the place of the saddle.

Now the sun was rising above the hills, shining warmly and comfortingly on the sleeping commando. The warmth and the rest were good for Daniel. The colour was already returning to his face.

But then the short penetrating sound of a trumpet was heard, the signal to saddle the horses, and the march was resumed, until the heads of the Biggarsberg mountains became visible. General Kock sent a few patrols ahead to scout out the mountain pass. When no sign of the enemy was found, the men traversed the narrow dangerous passes without hindrance. They rested only when it was absolutely necessary, and the march proceeded until evening fell and rain and darkness compelled them to stop.

It was a sombre night. They could not have fires because there was no wood, and there were no tents, for the ox wagons carrying the equipment could not keep up with the commando. The horses went hungry, for the *veld* was dry and bare, but the men were even worse off, and lay down in silence in the cold, pouring rain on the soggy ground.

Daniel suffered greatly that night, but bore up under the strain; every time he caught his father's compassionate look, a weak smile appeared on his face as if to say: "Don't worry, it will be all right!"

Louis had no problem. He had an iron constitution. He simply rolled himself up in his rain cloak and slept like a log. But most of the Boers couldn't sleep. They rose from their muddy beds and paced up and down despondently in an effort to get warm. Blikoortje followed their example. Stretching his stiff limbs, he called in an imperious voice, "Hey there — a hot toddy, and make it a stiff one, please!" at which his companions burst out laughing in spite of the miserable conditions.

It was still night when they quietly saddled the horses and before noon they reached the outskirts of Elandslaagte.

The advance guard of Kock's army had already reached Elandslaagte the day before. They had broken up the railway line in several places and captured an English provision train.

A Boer Commando on the way to Elandslaagte

It was a lovely day. The sun shone down from a cloudless sky. The Boers, who were now numb with cold, could indulge in food and drink, and could rest from all the hardship they had suffered.

That was the way things went in the war. It was full of excesses, ups and downs, and contradictions. One would sit in the saddle for twenty-four hours at a time, and then sleep for sixteen hours. On a certain day one would feel ready to give every last possession for one draught of water, and the following day seize a convoy of the enemy and drink like water the champagne destined for British officers. One day one would fight with the dogs for a bone to gnaw on, and the next day feast on tins of the finest salmon, taken at Dundee. Shortage and profusion, poverty and riches, hardship and pleasure — never do they alternate more often and more suddenly than in wartime!

To Blikoortje in particular everything was now all sunshine and prosperity. He had begun to get really hungry, and had started sniffing around like a hunting dog which had smelled game. And he had a very good nose, that Blikoortje! His hunt had not taken more than twenty minutes when he sat down with a number of hospitable Dutchmen who had joined this commando, to share their meal of ribs of mutton and drink foaming barley beer, while he entertained the company with his wonderful witticisms.

When he had taken his fill, he left his friendly hosts to look for his friends, the Wessels family. He stuck his hands in his pockets, whistling a merry tune, chased a cat that had done him no harm, and found his friends at the foot of a hill.

They had made a fire and brewed coffee over it, while on the ground next to the fire lay a bag with *biltong* and rusks prepared by Aunt Sannie. Master Wessels was in a cheerful mood. Daniel was eating the hard rusks with relish, and Louis, who had already eaten, lay sleeping with Pluto under his head for a pillow.

"Well, Blikoortje, have you had something?" asked Master Wessels. "We still have something left in the bag, my boy!"

"Thank you very much," answered the boy with dignity, "but I have had leg of mutton."

"Then you are better off than we," laughed Daniel. "Couldn't you help us to some leg of mutton too?"

"Leg of mutton I can't manage, but a roasted chicken may be possible," answered Blikoortje.

"Well, then, show us what you can do," said Daniel.

"Right!" answered the boy. He climbed the hill, at the foot of which the family was camping, cupped his hand around his mouth, and began to expertly imitate the cock-a-doodle-doo of a rooster.

But there was no reply.

He turned around and crowed in the opposite direction.

"Are you making any progress?" Daniel called from below.

"Done, my friend!" called out Blikoortje triumphantly. "I can hear him."

And indeed the crowing of a rooster could be heard in the distance. Daniel was so intrigued that he made haste to accompany Blikoortje on his hunt.

"There it is!" said Blikoortje after they had climbed over several ridges and an old farmhouse came into sight near a small stream.

The gate stood open and they both approached the front door. Everything looked deserted and very dismal. In front of the doghouse lay a chain and a dog collar, but there was no dog. Behind the house stood a cart with a broken axle, and on the ridge of the roof a few lone pigeons sat looking on inquisitively.

Blikoortje opened the unbolted door, and they entered the living room. The ashes were still warm in the grate, evidence that the residents had just fled. That it had been a hasty flight could be seen everywhere. The floor was covered in rags, old shoes, and discarded papers. In one corner stood an old chair with a sagging seat and broken rungs. Among the scattered straw bedding lay broken earthenware. There was a mirror lying next to the hearth. It had probably broken when taken from the wall, and was no longer worth taking along.

A cat that was slinking around the living room looked at the intruders with fearful eyes and fled outside.

Daniel and Blikoortje had had enough of the sight. They went out to the chicken run, built against one of the side walls of the house, and began to look for the rooster.

Unfortunately the chicken run was empty. On the ground stood a cracked earthen dish with muddy water. A few grains of barley lay scattered about.

Blikoortje looked at Daniel. "Nothing here!" he said ruefully.

But while he was looking around behind the house, he saw the longed-for rooster sauntering calmly over the dunghill.

"Now let me take aim like an expert," said Blikoortje. He put his rifle to his shoulder and put a bullet through the rooster's head. The bird did a double somersault with its wings spread, and then lay still with its legs stretched out stiffly.

Gijs Wessels looked up in amazement when he saw Blikoortje approaching with his loot in his hand. Quickly the rooster was plucked, slaughtered, and roasted on the spit.

What a meal that was! Daniel hadn't tasted anything like it for the past fourteen days.

Chapter XIII
The Eve of the Battle

Then came the morning of Saturday, October 21.

The Boer camps which had been pitched to the east of the railway line were moved farther back for safety's sake. But Elandslaagte with its roofs of blue corrugated iron was still visible, and between the green leaves of trees and shrubs the railway station could be seen.

There was only a little grass on the *veld*, so the Dutch volunteers were going to collect feed for the horses — sheaves of oats from the seized train. Six strong oxen were harnessed to the feed wagon. No one suspected the presence of the enemy until a smoke plume farther up the railway line betrayed the approach of an armoured British train.

There were three cars on the train, protected by slate-coloured steel plates against enemy fire. Between the front and the middle cars sat the locomotive, thus protected, while the last was an open car carrying a Maxim cannon.

On the freight road from Ladysmith to Elandslaagte, which took about six hours on foot, columns of cavalry and artillery were moving under Cavalry General French, to the left of the train, on the western side of the railway line. He had thoroughly reconnoitred the area to learn the position and strength of the enemy. He halted a thousand metres from the railway station, and had the cannon unhooked.

It was half-past seven in the morning when the first shot from British cannon thundered over the *veld*. It bored right through the freight depot into the ambulance wagon of the Boers. The second shot was aimed toward the open *veld*, in the direction of the Dutch camp, where the tent of commander Jan Lombaard, who led the Dutch Volunteers, drew their attention. The shell struck the ground twenty-five metres from the tent without exploding; the next bomb, landing some distance behind the tent did explode but wounded no one.

The Dutchmen forgot about their oats, which was wise; the two cannon which the Boers had brought along spewed their bombs very accurately into the English battery, which was just as wise.

General French felt that his seven-pounders were no match against this fire and ordered a retreat. With his men and the armoured train he withdrew a distance of one hour on foot and stopped at the railway station of Modderspruit.

Jan Kock now gave orders to seek contact with the enemy, and the Boers swarmed over the hills in small scattered groups on their tough little horses. Their horses climbed the different hills like mountain goats, finally reaching a high ridge of the mountain which gave an excellent view of the enemy's position. Through their field-glasses the Boers discovered three military trains on the railway line, and next to the railway the infantry battalions were spread out.

Outposts were set up, and at noon the Boers returned to their camp at a gallop. They were pleasantly surprised by the arrival of the transport wagons, bringing indispensable equipment for the camp from Volksrust: groceries, tents, refreshments, and a huge mail bag full of letters and newspapers.

There was also a letter for Gijs Wessels. He recognized the simple, somewhat cramped handwriting of his wife. Together with Daniel — Louis and Blikoortje had stayed at the outposts — he sat down behind a rock providing shelter from the wind to enjoy the letter. It ran as follows:

Dear Husband and Children!
    It was a really sad day when you left. Janske tried to bear up before me, but I could see that she was very sad. However, I found rest in the knowledge of God's providence, and the Lord brought to my attention the words: "What I am doing you don't understand now, but you will know after this."* It was a wonderful comfort to me, since I really took to heart the precious truth that all riddles will one day be solved. In this way I could turn over everything with childlike faith to the Lord who rules everything. It is true,

---

* John 13:7.

dear husband, that nothing can part us from the love that is in Jesus. It is exactly in these fearful and anxious times that we are comforted in a wonderful way by our God, and He has been our refuge from generation to generation! He will also make it good to our people. I firmly believe that one day we will have one great, free, united South Africa.

This morning I read with attention the sixth Psalm, and at the end I had to exclaim: "Poor England!" For they are assaulting God's children and spilling the blood of God's chosen people.

But often I am grieved, dear husband and children, when I think of you. Now we come to realize how much we mean to one another. I cannot see the large empty arm-chair, without becoming very upset, and at times I fall prey to a relentless fear. Is this a premonition that something terrible is going to happen? But it may be nothing more than my shattered nerves. I've known such fear before without anything happening and you laughed at me in the end. So we hope we will see one another in good health again. It is a just cause, dear husband and children, for which you are struggling. So fight bravely for your people and your country, for that is the will of the Lord!

We cannot see one another now, but it is my wish that we may meet again in good health. So I remain, with heartiest greetings,

Your loving Wife and Mother
S. Wessels, born Potgieter

P.S. One more thing. Dear Daniel, take good care, my boy, and don't exhaust yourself! If there is hard work to do, your brothers can surely help you. So goodbye, Daniel, goodbye, Louis, goodbye, Kees, goodbye, Karel, goodbye, my dear husband — I entrust you all to the Lord! Janske sends her heartiest regards. She hopes to write soon. Do not worry about us! The blacks are very obedient, and all is going well with the farming.

The same.

The letter was most invigorating to Gijs Wessels. Daniel had been sitting next to his father, leaning on his shoulder with his left arm so as to be able to read everything, and now his gentle eyes shone with tears.

Wessels looked at his son and noticed how pale he was.

"I should have left you at home, my son," he said. "I am afraid the campaign will be too hard on you."

Daniel stroked his father's careworn cheek lovingly.

"Don't worry," he said in a valiant voice, "I feel as strong as a young horse."

He smiled as he spoke, and put on a cheerful face to dispel the clouds on his father's brow.

But a father's love has a penetrating eye and is not easily misled. Gijs Wessels shook his head and sighed.

In the distance heavy cannon-fire could be heard. The Boer got up, climbed a hill, and stared toward the horizon.

Slowly he came back. His face was even more sombre than previously.

"We will be going into battle today, Daniel," he said quietly.

The boy leaped up.

"Are you not afraid, my son?"

"We are in the hands of the Lord."

"It may cost you your life, Daniel!"

"I gladly give my life for the freedom of my people."

His eyes shone as he spoke and his cheeks became flushed.

"Do you *dare* to die, Daniel?"

He had previously asked the same question, that last night before they had left *Wonderfontein*, but in the face of death and eternity, he felt he had to touch upon it once more. So old Wessels asked it with emphasis, and while asking, his eyes rested on his child in solicitous tension.

But Daniel lifted his gentle eyes without qualm to his father and calmly said, "I'm not afraid of death."

"Why not, Daniel?"

"I belong to Jesus, my Saviour, who has bought me with His precious blood."

He said this so simply, so artlessly. But it was precisely this simplicity that showed the immeasurable strength of his faith.

Still Gijs Wessels was not satisfied.

"You are still so young, Daniel, and yet you speak with such conviction. I have been on the journey for a long time, and still my soul is often swayed by doubt and fear."

But Daniel answered in a tranquil voice, "God has forgiven all my sins. He loves me. I know that for sure."

"Then all is well, my son!" said his father, and pressed Daniel's hand.

Once more the thunder of cannon could be heard in the distance, louder than before, heavy and threatening like thunder from an approaching storm. Over the hills the Boer scouts came swarming at full gallop, like albatrosses announcing a storm.

"Do you know where Louis is?" asked the old Boer.

"He was on the outpost just now," said Daniel.

"I would have liked to have him here," sighed Gijs Wessels.

He looked around to try to see the young hunter, but could not find him. He became very grave. He took Daniel by the hand, and brought him to a nearby thornbush.

"Let us kneel here, Daniel, and commend our souls to God."

So together they knelt, father and son, the thornbush shading them with its branches. Its yellow blossoms were fragrant, and from its branches flew a bird, which spread its wings and sang its song.

It was the last song sung that day above Elandslaagte.

They rose from their knees. Master Wessels's eyes were moist. He kissed his son on his brow. Daniel saw that his father was greatly moved.

"You mustn't be sad, dear Father," he said consolingly. "See — I am not alarmed!" Once again he smiled while speaking, but his lips trembled.

"You are still so very young," groaned the father. "But come on, Daniel, it is time!"

Chapter XIV
Elandslaagte

It was time.

Calmly and without haste, the commanders surveyed the positions through their field-glasses and saw the British infantry advancing in three gray-brown lines.

The trumpets gave the signal, and the burghers mounted quickly. They brought their horses behind the hills and left them in the care of black servants, and then scaled the hills.

Little was said. The seriousness of the situation and the uncertainty of the near future caused all hearts to beat faster.

In the meantime the enemy's artillery charged across the *veld*, and then opened fire. Eighteen British cannon flung their shells and grape-shot at the Boer position, striking the rocks behind which the Boers lay hidden.

Gijs Wessels' rifle was supported between two rocks. It rested there like a cannon on its mount. Daniel lay at his side.

Old Wessels peered over the rocks to the gray-brown lines slowly approaching over the undulating terrain. Now and then he gave his son an encouraging glance.

The boy was really very plucky. His lips were pursed, and he was trying to control the trembling that at times ran over his limbs like a fever, amid the hellish music of war.

"You have the cannon-fever, Sonny!" came a voice behind him, while a hand was laid on his shoulder. It was a forceful, courageous voice, which stood him in good stead at that moment.

"The cannon-fever — but it will get better, I tell you!"

"Louis," said Daniel as he looked behind him, "I'm glad you are here with us!"

Old Wessels also glanced over his shoulder, and when he looked the young hunter in the face, a mixture of love and parental pride lit up his gray eyes. Indeed! Other Afrikaans fathers might have had brave sons too, but there were few who could match Louis.

He had first noted Louis's fearless leonine nature almost four years ago at Krugersdorp, when a report had to be carried through a rain of enemy bullets. No one had dared to do it — but Louis. And his father's heart had quaked when the young hunter undertook the perilous ride. A neighbour had tapped him, the father, on the arm, saying, "Is that your son, Cousin Gijs? You can be proud of the boy, but it will be a fine day if you get him back with both his legs shot off." Louis had mounted calmly as if it were a hunting trip, and when he returned with a bullet through his hat but otherwise unharmed the burghers had erupted in a loud hurrah. But the young hunter had shaken his head in surprise and said, "I don't understand — have I done something unusual?"

"Stay with us now," said Gijs Wessels.

"Of course," returned Louis. "This is a good position for shooting Redcoats!" and he lay down on the other side, to the left of his father.

Master Wessels looked at him again. Louis had not been so cheerful in weeks. It seemed that the approaching clash relaxed him.

"Have you prayed, Louis?" his father asked in a grave voice.

The young hunter nodded in the affirmative.

"And what did you pray for, Louis?"

"That we may shatter the enemy, Father!"

"But did you also think of your own soul?" asked Master Wessels.

"I thought more of the Redcoats in my prayer than of myself," answered Louis frankly.

He rose a little from his reclining position and his face clouded over.

"What is this?" he cried, stamping the ground angrily. "Are those Boers fleeing? Ho, that Master Blijvenstein — the coward — he runs faster than all the others! Are all the Johannesburgers taking to their heels? Can't they stick to their positions?"

Suddenly he lowered the field-glasses he had in his hand.

"There are the Rednecks!" he called in a loud voice. "Stay, boys! There — there!"

He ran to another rock to get a better shot at the enemy.

Then the sound of gunfire could be heard behind the hills. The British had come within the Boers' line of fire.

Master Wessels threw another look at Daniel. The boy had overcome his cannon-fever. His face was glowing, his eyes shone, and the Mauser lay steady in his hands. The gentle, almost feminine appearance had suddenly gone from his face. At this moment he looked remarkably like the young hunter. The boy had ripened to a man in the heat of the battle and his mouth was set in a determined line.

"You must hit the mark, Daniel — not too fast!" said the father. "Go for the highest ones!"

"Do you see that tall officer, there, with the drawn sabre in his hand?" asked Daniel.

Master Wessels nodded.

"I'll get him!" said Daniel, putting his hand on the breech.

And indeed the tall officer tumbled to the ground, his sabre describing a semi-circle.

The Boers gave a terrible, furious rain of fire, but were unable to stop the fearful wall of enemies approaching like an unstoppable spring tide.

"It's no use," said a voice near Daniel.

"Is that you, Blikoortje?" asked Daniel.

"Yes, it's me!" answered the boy in anger while slamming five more bullets into the magazine of his Mauser.

"It's no use," he said once more. "If you pick off one of the Redcoats, another ten come for the funeral."

The British infantry were now spreading out wide, to escape the deadly fire of the Boer rifles; then they appeared on the ridge of a hill. Quickly they came down the other side to take up the next position, trampling underfoot the lilies lifting their friendly faces from the fresh green of the *veld*.

The English cavalry was swarming on the flanks in order to get around the Boers' position. From the Biggarsberg heavy clouds were closing in, forming a sombre background against which the light of exploding grenades stood out ominously.

The battle was nearing its climax, and it seemed as if the heavens were trying to quench the rage and fury of the humans with a torrent of rain. The clouds opened their sluices and it came pouring down. But the rage and the fury were not to be thus extinguished, and relentlessly the British pressed onward — uphill, downhill, twice staggering under the hail of Mauser bullets before the final rush.

Gijs Wessels looked at his son Daniel.

"How are you doing, my son?"

"Fine," said Daniel; "fine!"

The rigid tension on his face had softened; once again it was the gentle, friendly face of a child. But of anxiety or fear there was no sign.

"Not afraid, Daniel?"

"The LORD is with me — whom shall I fear?"

They were the last words Daniel spoke on earth.

Gijs Wessels heard a sigh — it was the sighing, whistling sound of a Lee-Metford bullet, and that sigh cut off the thread of his son's life. The bullet had gone through that young, kind heart, and death followed immediately.

At that very moment Louis came running.

"We have lost the battle," he called; "we must fall back. We are being surrounded!"

But he stopped short as if nailed to the ground.

"Daniel has gone home," said Gijs Wessels in a choked voice.

Louis bent down.

Daniel was bare-headed. His hat lay next to him. The black cock feather which Janske had stuck into his hat at their farewell had become red — the colour of blood.

With able hands Louis unfastened the shirt drenched in blood and bared the chest. He put his ear to Daniel's heart.

"Dead!" he cried. "He is dead!"

There was unspeakable accusation in that one word *dead*.

Fleeing Boers were passing them, stumbling over the stones, and tumbling to the foot of the hill.

It was terrible.

"Flee!" said Louis to his father. "I'll think of a way to bring him out."

"No," said old Wessels, "*you* must flee; I'll take care of Daniel."

He said it in that peculiarly kind but determined tone which demands obedience, but Louis could not find it in him to leave his father alone.

"They will take you captive, Father!"

"They won't take me captive; God will take care of me — now go!"

Then the young hunter threw his rifle over his shoulder, and went off. He hesitated once again, until his father gestured urgently for him to go. Then he hastened down the hill.

On his way he came upon Blikoortje who, in his eagerness to get the best position for shooting, had taken up a place far to the left.

Louis touched him on the shoulder. The boy gave him a quick glance.

"It's time to go!" said the young hunter.

"I have to pick off two more; then I'll have a full dozen," answered Blikoortje calmly.

"They'll take you prisoner — come on!"

"Two more — one more!" said the boy, pulling the trigger, putting a bullet through the head of an English officer at a distance of fifty yards.

"It's your decision," said Louis. He bounded down the hill, looking for his bay, which had fortunately remained unscathed, and then mounted. He threw the reins loosely over the horse's neck and guided him with the pressure of his knees, while Pluto, who had not left his side during the whole battle, ran ahead with fearful eyes.

Darkness was gathering fast. The heavy downpour had stopped, but it was still drizzling, and the bay horse, which had become wild under the unaccustomed and terrifying artillery fire, charged over the undulating plain.

The young hunter looked back.

The English trumpets were sounding for the last rush, one trumpeter taking over the signal from another. In the faint light Louis could see the shimmer of bayonets held aloft. The signal for the attack rang out again and yet again, and the tide of the British rose up against the hard rocks of the Boers — higher and higher — and broke over them with irresistible force!

Louis heard the jubilant cries of the Scottish Highlanders and the playing of their bagpipes. He laid his hand on his heart — it felt like it had been pierced with a razor-sharp knife.

Now from the right a huge dark shadow approached, and suddenly the ground seemed to tremble under the hooves of many horses.

"The lancers!" he groaned. "The lancers!"

They clashed with the right flank of the fleeing Boers whom he had passed on his fast horse. He heard fearful cries and pleas for pardon, and in between the command: "Wipe out the vermin!"

Four times the executioners rode through the ranks of the wretched Boers, their lances doing their dreadful work. The fugitives were struck down, the wounded murdered.

If Louis had continued, he would have been safe, but the horrible scenes behind him and concern for his father held him back.

He swerved to the left, into the *veld*, and in a wide curve approached the now-deserted battlefield at a walk.

The lancers had come together in small groups, swarming across the *veld* with their lances up, looking for fleeing Boers. Twice such a patrol, deceived by the dark and the fine drizzle, had galloped past the young hunter, but the third time he was noticed by a new patrol of four men, led by a black guide. They bore down on him, but he made no effort to escape.

And why would he? It would only have increased the danger, since the pursuers would call on other patrols to help them.

He took his rifle from his shoulder — the patrol was very near.

"Halt!" called the corporal. "Give up your gun!"

The young hunter didn't say a word, but at a distance of five paces put a bullet through the corporal's head.

At that very moment, however, the three other lancers, pressed toward him and would probably have pierced him with a lance, had he not escaped the danger by having his horse make a quick leap.

Once more he took aim, and the second lancer tumbled dying from the saddle.

Frightened by such unexpected opposition, the remaining two lancers had had enough. They spurred their horses on and disappeared into the darkness with the black man.

Louis jumped from his horse.

The corporal was already dead. His body still hung in the saddle, with his head hanging down. The horse was dragging the dead horseman along slowly, for it was hungry, and looking for green shoots of grass.

The other horse had taken flight with its lancer, slinging its rider along, all the while bashing his head on the sharp rocks.

Louis untangled the corporal's hands from the reins and freed his feet from the stirrups.

Then he examined the lance. The point with its little flag was coloured with fresh blood.

"This blood at least has been avenged," he mumbled through gritted teeth.

He removed the dead man's tailcoat.

"I'll put on this coat," he thought to himself, "and then I'll be safe on the battleground."

But an indescribable revulsion came over him, and he threw the coat on the ground. Just at that moment he could see another patrol approaching. There were at least ten men. What should he do? There was no time to think it over, and his desire to assist his father overcame his revulsion for the coat of a murderer.

Quickly deciding, he hastily pulled on the coat, and putting on the helmet, threw his own jacket over the corpse, and swung into the saddle.

The patrol was by this time quite near, but the officer in command was somewhat nonplussed on discovering the lancer.

"What are you doing here, Corporal?" he asked distrustfully.

"I am busy wiping out the vermin," answered the hunter calmly, pointing his foot in the direction of the corpse.

"But why are you out alone, Comrade?"

"Oh, well, they're only vermin, Lieutenant; I take on four of them."

The officer was reassured, and looked around to see if there were any fleeing Boers. But suddenly he fixed his gaze on the bay

The Boers slaughtered at Elandslaagte

horse on which Louis sat, and saw by his gear that he was not an English cavalry horse. His suspicion arose anew.

"Why are you riding a Boer horse, man?"

"Because this Boer horse is in considerably better condition than that skinny horse grazing over there!"

The lieutenant peered into the gloom once more, and thought he saw a few fleeing shadows. He pointed his sabre in the direction of the shadows, and spurred his horse on.

The lancers followed him.

"Shouldn't I have the corpse buried?" Louis called after him.

"Buried?" laughed the officer, turning in the saddle for a moment. "It's only vermin, and the scavengers must also have something!"

"I agree!" said the young hunter wholeheartedly, and leaving the corpse behind on the open *veld*, he rolled up his own coat and hat, bound them to his saddle, and rode away in the direction of the battlefield.

After Louis had left in obedience to his father's command, the English had quickly neared. Master Wessels laid down Daniel in a protected spot.

He once more took up his rifle, for he knew his duty. There were no more than thirty burghers left in that position, but this small Gideon's band held high the honour of the whole Afrikaans nation and fought with the same courage as the Spartans of old.

Death gathered a rich harvest. One soldier clutched above his head as though looking for invisible support to hold him up; the next fell backward as though struck by lightning, staining the hard rocks with his blood; just beyond, a big Scottish Highlander reared like a horse gone wild, fell sideways, and grasped at the grass, his stiffening hands trying to hold on to the sinking earth.

But no matter how many died, the British courage stormed forward, and fixing bayonets on their rifles, they scrambled up to the Boers' positions. Enemy bullets screamed over the hill.

Gijs Wessels put his hand to his head; then he saw the bloodstain on his hand — blood was streaming down his face.

He held onto a rock so as not to fall, but a darkness fell over his eyes — bayonet points were dancing madly before his eyes. He sat down, and his last look fell on his child who had passed away.

When he recovered consciousness, he knew that the end was near.

It was already quite dark, for it was raining softly, and evening had come.

He called to a passer-by.

"What do you want?" asked the man, a British officer with a stern face.

"My child who has died — bring him to me!" he pleaded in a breaking voice, and with a last effort of his waning strength he stretched out his hand to the right where he thought Daniel was.

The officer was not as harsh as his strict face would have one think. He took the trouble to look until he found Daniel among a number of corpses, and laid him carefully in the arm of his father.

Gijs Wessels clasped his beloved son close to his heart. He gave the British officer a look of extreme gratitude.

Then he closed his eyes.

Thus he passed away peacefully — the master of *Wonderfontein*, with his sleeping child in his arms.

Chapter XV
Father and Son

The small major was standing deep in thought by the two lifeless bodies when he saw the figure of a tall, powerfully built lancer approaching.

The lancer was walking slowly. He seemed to be looking for something. Every now and again he called in a subdued voice: "Search, Pluto, search!"

As the faithful animal came near the officer, he let out a long drawn-out, plaintive whine. In two, three paces the lancer reached his dog — it was standing next to two corpses.

Then he glanced around as a hand was laid on his shoulder.

"Louis Wessels!" said a voice.

He had been recognized. An anxious expression appeared on the young hunter's face as he looked into the eyes of the small major.

He had seen this officer before, but where had it been? He tried to remember — oh yes, he knew — in the home of Arend Uys that fateful afternoon.

"Allow me to take leave of my father and my brother first," he said calmly.

The major said nothing. He seemed to nod slightly.

Yet for Louis Wessels, as he bent over his dead, there was no major about to take him prisoner, and no danger concerned him.

He knelt beside his father and brother and gazed at them long and fervently, with eyes blinded by tears.

It was a poignant picture of peace that lay before him. They seemed to be sleeping! No bitterness of death overshadowed their features. Instead, their faces were full of a quiet, gentle peace. That was not strange. For Gijs Wessels had often said: "The LORD gives it in their sleep to those He loves," and now they had received it in their sleep. And the quiet peace on their faces — what else could it be but a reflection of the everlasting, indescribable bliss their souls had entered on crossing the threshold of eternity?

The rain began to fall faster again. At a distance the murderers who belonged to the fifth lancers' regiment were galloping past.

The young hunter took a cloth and spread it over the faces of Gijs Wessels and his son Daniel. He did it carefully as though he was afraid of waking them. Before his eyes he seemed once more to see the scene — so recently — when he had also spread a cloth over their faces. Then it had been the sun which might have bothered them in their sleep, but he had not been careful enough, for they had awakened. Now no sun bothered them, but cold, drizzling rain beat on their faces. So Louis spread the cloth over their faces with tender care.

A few paces away lay Daniel's hat. Louis took from it the nice black cock feather, which was red with blood.

The young hunter was deeply moved, but still amazingly calm. He had seen other corpses on the battlefield, with fists clenched in the last struggle of death; faces drawn with intolerable and unspeakable pain; eyes opened wide in death as if they had seen something unspeakably horrible.

But here, in his father and his brother, there was no trace of the like. For them death had no terror. They were at rest.

He rose up, looking into the stern face of the small, silent major.

"A friendly hand has laid my brother in the arms of his father," he said.

"I did," said the major. "It was your father's last wish — he was your father, wasn't he?"

Louis nodded, and gripped the hand of this extraordinary man.

"I am sincerely grateful to you, Major!"

A few spades were lying nearby. Some black men with lanterns were crossing the battlefield.

"May I call them, Major? I would very much like to give my father and my brother an honourable burial."

The major himself called the black men, and Louis gazed without words at the hands which quickly dug the grave.

So in that quiet spot they were gently laid to rest — father and son, Daniel in the arms of the master of *Wonderfontein*.

Louis piled hard rocks over the grave. Now his beloved ones were safe from the vultures that fed on the corpses and the wild animals that violated the battlefields.

Only then did he think of himself again. He was a captive, and although he set a high price on his freedom he did not want to gain it by using his weapons. He felt defenceless against the magnanimity of the small major, and rising, he said, "Now I am at your disposal."

But there was no one to hear these words. The major had gone, giving the captive his freedom.

So he was free. Accompanied by his dog, he pursued his way to the east.

A creaking ox wagon came along, full of soldiers and captives. The soldiers were shouting and singing, but the captives sat in the straw looking very downcast. On the front of the wagon, on a bale of straw, tied hand and foot, sat Blikoortje.

The young hunter recognized him. "I warned him," he said sadly, "but now it's too late."

He had fastened his horse to a willow tree earlier. Now he swung into the saddle and spurred his horse.

The tumult of the battle grew quiet. Only an occasional shot was now heard.

Suddenly the bay was spooked, and Pluto began to bark loudly and vigorously. The young hunter caught at the reins and halted.

To his right near a dry ditch sat a wounded man, who stretched out his hands in an urgent plea: "Spare me! I have a wife and seven small children!"

Then Louis jumped down, a flaming blush spreading over his cheeks.

"I cannot wear this murderer's costume any longer," he groaned, and taking off the lancer's coat and helmet, he threw them away with a vengeance, as though they were the clothes of one infected by the plague.

"You are not in danger," he said to the wounded man kindly. "See, I am your brother!"

He knelt down next to him, gave him a few draughts from his flask and bandaged his wounds.

"Where are you from?" asked Louis.

"From the Free State, Cousin. We were fighting with eighty men with your commando, but I have lost my comrades."

"Will you be able to ride on horseback without help?"

"If only I had a horse!"

"There's bound to be one that we could nab," said Louis, and unbelievably, he was able to catch a horse wandering loose.

The wounds of the Free Stater were only flesh wounds, and having been helped into the saddle by Louis, he rode on at a steady pace with him in a north-easterly direction.

It was late afternoon when they discovered a black man's hut on the open *veld*, dismounted, and entered.

There was not a soul to be seen, but inside the meagre abode lay some bundles of straw, which the young hunter spread out for his exhausted comrade who soon fell into a peaceful, refreshing sleep.

But Louis couldn't sleep. Scenes from the terrible day behind him arose before his overstrung mind. Bloody figures wringing their hands stood before him, and the dying cries of fugitives were drowned out by roars from lanced and spurred murderers.

Then gradually the horrible figures faded. The roars died down and lovely scenes appeared before his eyes. Again he was standing next to the two who had passed away. They were resting in each other's arms, and two angels were standing by them, one at the head, and the other at the feet. Their wings were spread out over the dead, so that none would disturb their rest. For they had not died — no, they were asleep . . .

But soon even this vision faded — the young hunter saw nothing more, heard nothing more, and he fell into a deep sleep without dreams.

Chapter XVI
Caught

Louis Wessels felt marvellously rested. Standing in front of the rotten threshold of the hut, he stretched his muscular limbs and breathed in full draughts of the fresh morning air.

The Free Stater was still asleep. Louis covered him with a sheepskin which lay rolled up against the wall of the hut. Then he went outside and made his way to a creek which was streaming through steep banks nearby. He drank from the cool water and refreshed himself.

He looked around. The morning sun shone in the blue sky, kissing the petals of the small wildflowers. Some way off a black man was herding his sheep, and from the mountain valleys white mist rose.

Out there, in the south-west — that had to be Elandslaagte. It seemed as though an eternity lay between the battle of Elandslaagte and this morning, yet it had been only a few hours. The strange, formidable events had given the minutes the meaning of hours, and it seemed to Louis that he had aged ten years in one night.

He had to think hard what day it was — oh, it was Sunday! Usually on this day his father would read a sermon, and Daniel would play the little harmonium, and the singing of Psalms would be heard rising from *Wonderfontein*.

Once more he glanced around, and was surprised. He felt convinced he had been there before. Yes, he have been — there was the winding dusty road with its deep potholes and steep heights, the transport road linking the railway line with the home of Arend Uys.

To the left of the road he saw a small house. He had once been there with Truida Uys. No, this was not that little house, because he had picked a flower from the garden there and given it to Truida, and in front of this little house there was no garden.

He took up his field-glasses. Yes, now he discovered the little house he was thinking of. It was quite near a high hill, and the flowers were once again blooming in the garden in front of the little house. Half an hour's travel farther, the dense trees among which the house of Arend Uys lay hidden could be seen. Between Arend Uys' house and that little house stood the new house, built for the young couple . . .

The young hunter abruptly lowered the field-glasses, and looked in a different direction.

The Free Stater was now standing next to him.

"How are you this morning?" asked Louis in friendly concern.

"I will be all right, Cousin," the Free Stater answered confidently. "I merely had two dumdum bullets, one in my right shoulder, and one in my left arm. I will be all right, Cousin, but I would really have liked a cup of coffee!"

Louis was quite prepared to help his comrade.

"Are we a long way from the road, Cousin?"

"We're in the middle of nowhere," answered Louis. "Over there is the transport road."

They returned to the hut, but all of a sudden the young hunter stopped short.

"Have you seen anyone in the vicinity?" he asked, but the Free Stater shook his head.

"I thought I just saw somebody disappearing behind the hut."

"It must have been one of our horses, Cousin. They are grazing behind the hut," the Free Stater answered reassuringly.

They both entered the hut. The saddle lay next to the fireplace. A coffee kettle and a leather bag with ground coffee were tied to the saddle with a strap. Louis quickly kindled a fire and filled the kettle with water, and the coffee was soon made. A tin mug served as a cup and the Boers took turns sipping the hot black coffee. Louis also shared his dry bread with his new friend like a brother, and soon the Free Stater was feeling very good.

But then he wanted to go. The young hunter helped him to saddle his horse while the Free Stater thanked him profusely for his help.

"Keep due north," warned Louis, "so that you don't fall into the hands of the Rednecks!"

He also saddled his own horse, whistled for his dog, and turned to the Waschbank.

From the bushes right next to the hut, a patrol of six lancers appeared. They were accompanied by a Zulu.

"There he goes — our bird has flown!" cried one of the lancers.

"Never fear," said the sergeant. "I wish I was as certain of the Victoria Cross as I am of this Boer."

"It is him, isn't it?" he asked of the Zulu riding next to him.

"Oh yes, it's him, Master," said the black man with conviction. "I followed him last night in the dark, and I looked at him while he slept. I was so near to him I could feel his breath. I was tempted to thrust this steel" — he pointed to a long broad knife which he carried in a sheath on his belt — "between his ribs."

"Then you would not have gotten the promised reward," said the sergeant calmly, "for we must have him alive. Come on, men!"

By now Louis Wessels had caught sight of his pursuers. He was not unduly worried, and spurred his horse on so that the distance dividing them was increasing visibly.

"He'll escape!" called out the lancers, spurring on their horses to the utmost. But the bay of the young hunter was a finely-bred horse; he threw back his beautiful head and left the pursuers far behind.

From the right, however, another patrol was nearing which tried to outflank the hunter. Things were now becoming serious, and Louis pressed the spurs deep into his horse's flanks. He flew over the *veld*, so that it almost seemed as if his hooves were not touching the ground.

"He'll still get away!" said one of the lancers.

"Oh no, he won't," replied another, reaching the top of a hill. "He will be trapped against that wide gorge over there."

"I suspect he will risk the jump over the gorge!" said the first lancer.

"He'll break his neck if he does!" said the second, shifting a piece of chewing tobacco between his brown teeth.

"He would rather break his neck than fall into your little hands," retorted the first, but the sergeant said calmly, "He won't escape us, boys — the trap has been laid!"

The young hunter now had pursuers behind him and to his right. He had already seen the gorge some time ago, and turned to the left where the gorge was narrower.

The first patrol came straight after him over the *veld*, and as he had to make a curve to reach the point where the gorge was at its narrowest, the distance between him and the first patrol was diminishing perceptibly.

But then he reached the desired point. He forced the horse backward, tightened the reins, and in a majestic leap the noble animal had cleared the gorge.

"There he goes," shouted the lancers with a British oath. "He has escaped after all!"

"Saved," cried the young hunter, "saved!"

But the words died on his lips, for twenty strong black hands took hold of him and pulled him off his horse.

"What do you say now, boys?" asked the sergeant with a laugh.

"You are a confounded fellow!" laughed the lancers, rubbing their hands with glee.

The sergeant now knew for certain that he had the right man. One of the lancers had confirmed the allegation made by a Zulu that this Boer had killed two British soldiers, a corporal and a common lancer. It was clear that he deserved a bullet for that, but before executing the sentence, the men should have a little fun with the captive. The lancers had actually gone to a lot of trouble to lay hands on this dangerous and cunning Boer who had put on the coat of a lancer to outwit the British, and they might as well have something for their trouble. That was what the sergeant thought, and the sergeant should know.

He took over the captive from his black allies, and had him taken to the edge of the woods where his feet were tied securely to the thick trunk of a tree.

With calculated cruelty, the sergeant had Louis' rifle laid down near him, not more than four paces away.

"What are you going to do?" asked Louis.

"We'll tell you soon," laughed the sergeant. "Come, boys, first we'll have a bite to eat!"

Breakfast was prepared, and instead of coffee they had whiskey. The lancers were very pleased with themselves, and with every sip they took from the flask they did not neglect to curse the Boers.

The young hunter looked at his rifle. There it was, at a distance of four paces, and to him that rifle meant life — freedom — everything . . .

A kind of furious rage came over him — rescue lay at a distance of four paces. There were still five live bullets in the magazine — enough to take out five men. And the sixth and last — he would knock him over the head with the butt!

He bent forward slowly and stretched out his hands — he made a desperate but futile attempt to free his feet, but stopped when that met with roars of laughter from the enemy.

As the furious rage died down he was moved by deep sorrow. He realized how great the disaster was that had broken over the flourishing family at *Wonderfontein*. His father and his brother were resting in their cold grave and he, the eldest son of the family had become a defenceless target for ridicule and scorn. He sat down next to the tree trunk to which his feet were bound, and covered his face.

"Show us your mug!" called a lancer.

"He's beginning to cry!" mocked the black man.

"Quiet, boys, he's praying!" taunted the sergeant.

The black man had been right — Louis was crying, and the sergeant had also been right when he said, "Quiet, he's praying."

The lancers got up from the ground.

"Mount your horses, boys," commanded the sergeant. "Now we are going to do some target practice!"

He turned toward their captive.

"Get up, Boer, and make your last will!"

Louis did not move. He kept his hands before his face. He could not permit the enemy the triumph of seeing that his heart was deeply moved.

The sergeant did not make any effort to get him to stand up. With his pocket knife he carved a mark in the tree, five inches above the head of the prisoner.

"This is your target, boys — this mark on the tree. Be careful not to hit the Boer! It would be a shame if he died before his time!"

The lancers took out their revolvers, but none even hit the tree.

"Boys, you really are pathetic shots today!"

"It would be better with the lance, Sergeant!"

"Of course, the way it was last night — advance one horse length!"

The patrol shortened the distance to the prisoner by one horse length.

"I will now show you, boys, how to shoot. Pay attention. Charles, I say, pay attention!"

"Sergeant," said Charles, stretching out his hand to the adjacent woods, "there — there . . ."

"So, what about it?" said the sergeant, quite composed. "I tell you, pay attention!"

Chapter XVII
The Afrikaans Girl

Truida Uys had not slept all night. She had not even gone to bed.

The day before, Saturday, she had first thought that there was thunder in the west, but later she heard from some blacks passing by that a heavy battle was being fought at Elandslaagte. Then she had sent Christiaan, her clever young Zulu servant, to gather information, directing him to take the fastest horse in the stable.

In the middle of the night he had returned, and in his simple language full of metaphors he had made a moving report on the horrors of the battle. In order to be better informed he had offered his services as a carrier after the battle, and he had heard from another black man how a Boer with a long gray beard and his son had been buried in the same grave.

"They lay next to each other like a sheep and its lamb," the Zulu had said.

"Do you know who they were, Christiaan?"

The black man looked at his mistress with sad eyes and answered, "His name was Wessels."

"Wessels," she said. "Surely it wasn't Gijs Wessels?"

He had hesitated to make a reply.

"And his son — was it his eldest son, Christiaan?"

"No," he answered, quite sure of himself, "it was not the eldest."

"How do you know that?" she shot back.

"I myself helped to bury them, Mistress — the old man and the young Master Daniel."

"Didn't you say just now you had heard it from other black men?" queried Truida.

"I meant to spare you," said the Zulu, "but I can't hide anything from you. Your eyes are like sunbeams that make the darkness light."

"And are you sure you are not mistaken?" asked Truida fearfully. "It was dark, and there was a drizzle, you said."

"It was not that dark, Mistress. I could recognize their faces — Daniel lay dead in his father's arm."

"Dead!" Truida had groaned. "Dead!"

But with an effort she had regained control of her emotions. "Were there any other people you knew?"

"No one except Major Courtney and a very tall lancer."

"Major Courtney — the one who comes here so often?"

"The very same, Mistress. He looked just as strict as always."

"What was the lancer doing there, Christiaan?"

"He took a rooster feather from the young one's hat and took it for himself."

"Quiet, please," she said. "I don't understand this." She rubbed her forehead, deep in thought.

"Did you not see him?" she asked — "*him*?"

The Zulu had looked at her with his sharp black eyes.

"You mean young Master Louis Wessels, Mistress?"

"Yes, that's who I mean," she said slowly.

"I did not see him," answered Christiaan.

"Then you may go," she had said in a fatigued voice. "You have done well, Christiaan."

So she had remained sitting by herself, her tired head resting on her hand.

She thought and thought, and a thousand suspicions tortured her wretched brain.

A rooster announced the morning in a loud voice, but she did not stir. The blacks were crossing the yard to take the cattle out of the *kraal*, but she never even heard them.

She opened the blinds — the sun was high in the sky. She blew out the lamp, and closed her eyes for a moment, for they were aching.

The old housekeeper approached, shuffling her feet as usual, looked into the room and asked whether Cousin Truida was coming to breakfast.

The girl shook her head.

"I am ill," said she. "I beg you, please let me alone!"

At ten o'clock the housekeeper once more appeared, but the big hunting dog of Louis Wessels rushed past her, bouncing onto Truida with wild leaps.

"There — I don't know what to do with the ugly beast!" cried the housekeeper. "He is mad, Cousin, stark, raving mad. He jumps up against all the doors with his dirty paws — don't look at me in such a strange way! I believe we shall all go mad here!"

But Truida could no longer stand it.

She took the housekeeper by the hand, and showed her out of the room.

"I believe one of us already is mad," said the housekeeper, looking wide-eyed at her cousin.

"You have never been in your right mind," said Truida with unusual acerbity. "Now go!"

So there she sat. Pluto laid his front paws on her knees and looked at her with eyes that would melt a stone.

The dog knew where Louis Wessels was. Was he still alive? Or was he already lying under hard stones?

If only the dog could speak!

Truida clenched her hands to her pulsating temples. Now she was really fearing insanity.

She had suffered a great deal in the last weeks, not the least during these morning hours. What the young Zulu had told her — that the lancers had murdered the defenceless wounded in cold blood — had filled her young soul with indescribable repugnance. But some time ago already, shortly after that fateful day when Louis had turned his back on her in rage, she had come to understand the hypocrisy and the wicked meanness of Chamberlain's policy and had turned away from it in horror.

It was bound to happen. The day had to dawn when the blindfold would be ripped from the eyes of this true daughter of the old *Voortrekkers* — and now the day had come!

It was true, Louis had acted wrongly in coupling his love for her so closely with his love for his fatherland. If he had acted more gently the breach would probably never have occurred. But did she reproach him for that? Was she cross with him? Oh, how could she be cross with him?

And here was his dog, with his paws on her knees. She stroked his shaggy head.

"Poor animal!" She burst out in passionate weeping. "We are both so unhappy!"

Then abruptly she stood up. Like a shaft of lightning a thought crossed her brain. She stared into the dog's big, plaintive eyes.

"Where is your master, Pluto?" she asked in a loud, penetrating voice. "Your master, Pluto? Tell me!"

And indeed he told her. Not in human language, but in gestures that could well be understood.

He took the pleats of her summer frock in his broad mouth, and pulled her with gentle force to the door — through the hallway — outside.

Old Manasse was just exiting the stable.

"Saddle my Basotho pony, Manasse," she ordered; "quickly!"

She hurried quickly inside again. Courage, determination, and new hope could be read in her every movement. Above the bedroom door hung her rifle, a beautiful carbine. She took down the weapon and inspected the lock. The polished steel of the barrel shone in the sunlight.

In the hallway she met the housekeeper.

"Forgive me for being so rude," said Truida.

The old woman did not understood, and was at a complete loss.

"Are you going out, Truida? Have something to eat first, Cousin Truida. Your breakfast is still on the table!"

Eat! Who could think of eating? Swift as a gazelle the young girl went out through the hallway, slung the rifle over her shoulder, and mounted.

Pluto was watching her with his intelligent eyes.

"Now, Pluto," she said, "show me the way! Come on, to your master! I'll follow you through fire and water!"

She had already disappeared from sight when old Master Uys, who had been visiting a native settlement, entered the house.

"Oh Cousin!" burst out the housekeeper. "What terrible times we live in! I've never seen Truida like this! She has gone off like a madman — and this being Sunday, too — I don't understand it!"

"Don't worry, Cousin!" said Arend Uys. "Be still. Everything will work out all right!" and he took up his old Dutch Bible.

Chapter XVIII
Reconciled!

"Sergeant," said Charles, stretching out his hand to the adjacent woods, "there — there . . ."

"So, what about it?" said the sergeant, quite composed. "I tell you, pay attention!"

The sergeant took aim with the revolver, and squeezed the trigger.

Actually it was not a bad shot — three inches below the mark he had cut; narrowly missing the head of the young hunter, the bullet went into the trunk.

"It could have been a better shot, boys, but my mount is somewhat troublesome today because of the flies. He won't stand still — Hallo! What is that?"

In the adjacent woods branches began snapping as though a deer was breaking through it with huge leaps. The next moment a huge dog made its appearance, followed by a woman on horseback. It was clear that she had ridden fast; the dog's tongue was hanging from his broad mouth, and the pony stood with trembling flanks.

Truida dismounted and took in the whole situation with one glance.

"Get up, Louis!" she called. "Up!"

Taking a knife, she cut through the ropes with which his feet were bound, and the next moment she pressed his rifle into his hand.

It all happened in a few seconds, so astonishingly fast that the lancers hadn't even thought to use their weapons.

But the sergeant hadn't lost his cool for a moment, and quickly levelled his revolver at the plucky girl.

"I warn you!" he called.

Her only answer was to lift her own carbine.

He pressed the trigger, and the bullet grazed her ear.

But then it was her turn and she didn't hesitate. How could she hesitate, this true daughter of the old *Voortrekkers*?

A short jet of fire flashed from her shining carbine, and the sergeant would have toppled from the saddle, had not two of the lancers supported him.

Courage and strength rushed through the young hunter's heart now that he was clasping his Mauser in his strong hands. But his first glance was not to the enemy, but to the heroic daughter of Arend Uys.

She stood proud and erect with the smoking carbine in her hands, cheeks pale and flashing eyes kept on the enemy, jeopardizing her own life to save what was dearest to her heart.

The foremost lancer reached for his sharp-pointed lance.

"Drop the lance!" she called out, taking aim again.

The young hunter had already aimed his rifle, and slowly the lance sank to the ground.

"Off with you!" said Louis to the soldiers. "Your lives will be safe, but be quick about it!"

But the sergeant had to remain behind, for he was dead. The lancers laid him on the ground for the black to bury. Then they turned their horses and rode off, first at a walk, looking back with misgiving once and again, but then at full gallop.

"Well, what do you make of that?" asked the first lancer, when they knew they were safe.

"We will have to return empty-handed," said the second.

"She looked as if she was possessed by the devil!" was the third one's opinion.

"Our sergeant could not escape his fate," the fourth offered as consolation. "I myself was there when a fortune teller in Durban read his palm and she said that a woman would be his downfall."

"Old wives' tales!" said Charles. "Nothing but old wives' tales! I did warn the sergeant, but he was too obstinate to listen. There you have it — he couldn't save his own skin!"

"I wish my mother in England had her promising youngest son back home," said the first lancer. "What a country! That girl is a shrew — come on, old nag, before I kill you with my lance!"

The black man had loaded the sergeant onto the horse. He would bury him behind the hill.

Now Louis and Truida were alone.

The girl sat down on the fallen trunk of a willow tree and Louis on the hard ground next to her. Pluto stretched himself out before their feet fully realizing that he had done his duty. He looked from one to the other, snapping at the flies humming around his head.

"Truida!" said Louis tenderly. "You have saved my life, my dearest!"

"I would be willing to give my life-blood to save your life," answered Truida. "Do you believe it, my love?"

"Yes," answered Louis, "I believe it!"

They were reconciled, bound to each other more closely than ever before. The rift which had come between them in one fateful moment had been only a sad misunderstanding, one which was consumed like a thin thread in the blazing fire of their love. Their hearts had found each other again. Never would they part again, and their faces reflected the joy of their reunion.

Yet their joy was not untainted. A cloud of sorrow darkened it and Elandslaagte threw its sombre shadow.

"Do you know about my father and Daniel, Truida?" he asked.

She nodded sadly.

"Were you the lancer who stood at their grave?" she asked suddenly.

"That was me!"

"My poor boy!" said she, her heart flooded with compassion.

She leaned over him, taking his face between her hands, and said in a stifled voice, "Let us find comfort in God!"

Near the woods could now be heard the hooves of many horses. It was a detachment of Boers, the vanguard of a huge commando, storming past at full gallop.

They were young people, full of pluck and spirit, longing to avenge Elandslaagte on the British.

They were laughing and joking, and the officer, who recognized Louis, waved his broad-brimmed hat, calling, "Remember, we first have to chase the Khakis into the sea before you can celebrate your wedding!"

"A wedding!" Truida said pensively. "I don't want a wedding as long as the poor Afrikaans nation is bleeding from a thousand wounds!"

This was a revelation to Louis. So now they really were one. Both had their feet firmly on the eternal pillars of freedom, truth, and justice.

"Oh Truida!" he cried. "Now we understand one another. Now you belong to our small band who bear the love for our nation like a flame. God Himself has lit that flame in your heart — you will taste it in all its sweetness and all its sorrow!"

"Oh Louis!" she said in an emotional outburst. "My hero and my knight! If only I could accompany you on the battlefield, to bind up your wounds and be with you when the bullet goes through your chest!"

"Don't be so fearful, Truida," he comforted her. "Do I look like one who has been earmarked for death?" He stretched his strong muscles — a picture of young, virile strength.

But then he was silent, for at Elandslaagte strong young heroes had fallen like grass before a mower. And in the distance the sound of rifles firing and the thunder of cannon, roaring for prey could be heard once again . . .

Chapter XIX
Blikoortje's Adventure

Evening was drawing near. A group of Boers were sitting around a campfire.

They belonged to the vanguard of the commandos of Lukas Meyer and Erasmus. After the occupation of Dundee on Sunday, October 22nd, they had chased off the exhausted battalions of General Yule.

"Blikoortje, now tell us how you escaped from the Rednecks!" said a young Boer.

Blikoortje was very flattered by this request. It was not necessary to ask him a second time to relate his marvellous escape in vivid colours.

"Well, then, listen, boys," he said, "and I'll tell you. Last Saturday at Elandslaagte I was rather obstinate. I was very disappointed that we would be beaten and I couldn't get over it. I decided to take out at least twelve Redcoats. Well, I had ten, Kees, when your brother Louis tapped me on the shoulder and warned me that it was time to go. I said, 'I must have two more, then I'll be off.'

"In the end I did get one more, although he was a scrawny one, but then I knew that the twelfth one would have to be shelved for later on, for I had fired my last bullet, and the Redcoats were springing from the ground like toadstools. I saw them everywhere: before me, behind me, beside me — and then I cleared out.

"Of course I wanted to reach my pony, a stubborn beast, but what do you know? A bomb came down just in front of his nose. Before my mind's eye I could see him flying into the air. But don't you fear! The bomb did nothing, and the pony probably thought it was a new form of feed. At least, he nibbled at the bomb with his long yellow teeth, and looked as if he would eat it like rye bread.

"I said: 'Come on, little beast, that's not food for you!' but at that very moment there came a second bomb, a really nasty one, that threw me to the ground. When I was up again, I still had in my hands the reins of the forepony, so to speak, but the afterpony had been blown away! Then I started running, you know, for I still had enough brains to know that it was not a very healthy situation.

"I ran as fast as I could, but the cavalry was on my heels, and coming nearer. Of course it's as plain as a pikestaff, one can't win against a big horse. But I still didn't feel like surrendering, and when the trooper cried, 'Stand still, you lout, or I'll shoot!' I became completely ornery. Then he took his bullet-spout and a bullet whistled past my ears. So I halted for the sake of peace, and put up my ten commandments.

"He was on me quite fast, and I looked at him in astonishment, for I was sure I had seen that moth-eaten face before.

" 'Give up your weapons!' he shouted in a frightful voice, and when I heard the voice, all my doubts were lifted, for it was certainly moth-eaten Janus with whom I had worked for a full ten months at a horse-dealer in Pieter-Maritzburg.

"I said, 'Janus, shake hands, old fellow — how are you?' "

Blikoortje made a very effective pause when he had reached this tense moment. The Boers were listening with relish, and the sociable raconteur threw an old rotten plank on the fire so that the flames flared up.

"Janus's face was priceless. He never was one of the brightest, and he looked at me completely dumbfounded. For a moment I thought of jumping into the saddle with him, and bringing moth-eaten old Janus with his skinny nag over to the side where freedom and justice are to be found. But I didn't dare to do it for the place was swarming with murderous lancers and dragoons, and I handed over my rifle.

" 'Janus, do you still not know me?' I asked, and truly — then he knew me.

" 'You are Blikoortje,' he said with a laugh.

" 'So why did you chase me until I was out of breath, Janus?' I asked. 'I'll tell your mother when I see her, my friend!'

" 'How can I help it?' he said a little irritably. 'It's war, man!'

" 'Yes, but this whole war is rubbish,' I said, 'and all of us should be locked up in an asylum for killing each other like this — why did you shoot at me, Janus? I'd like to know!'

"He just shrugged his shoulders.

" 'I did it just for diversion, Blikoortje!'

" 'But you could easily have killed me, Janus!'

" 'Oh no, Blikoortje, I shot past you. I did not want to hit you.'

"That was a lie, of course.

" 'You shouldn't speak like that, Janus,' I said with emphasis. 'I saw how you aimed at me with your bullet spout. So this is all the thanks I get for all those nice cups of coffee with sugar that you consumed at my mother's house. People are mean, Janus, really awfully mean!'

"He was quite impressed by what I had said, and I began to hope that he would let me off the hook for old times' sake. Just then around the hill came an infantry patrol. Well, then things became crazier. They took me along, and when I moved in the direction of making my escape they trussed me up securely and dumped me on the front seat of an ox wagon.

"When we had travelled a while, and my limbs were torn apart by the bumping of the miserable wagon, they halted. I was brought into a small tent, in the pleasant company of one corporal and two Highlanders and a small bucket of gin.

"By now it was night and one of the Highlanders said, 'My body is aching — I must have something to chase off the worms!' And he took a swig. The other one said, 'What a climate this place has! I'll die if I don't have a swig too.' And he did the same. So they competed in drinking — no, to tell the truth, boozing. And then they fell over, as drunk as lords.

"I thought to myself: 'Blikoortje, perhaps the corporal may also start drinking.' But no. He was on the water wagon, you know. Anyhow, it was quite dark in the tent. The only light we had was a mere pinprick from a dented lantern. However, I discovered a jagged peg nailed into the ground, and on this I slowly filed through the ropes on my hands.

" 'What's that scraping noise I hear?' asked the corporal. He was terribly suspicious.

"I answered calmly: 'Oh, that must be mice smelling the canvas of the tent.'

" 'Mice,' he said contemptuously but stammering a little, for he was not a fast speaker. 'Mice! Go tell that to the marines!'

" 'There it is again!' he said after a while, but I had just filed through the last thread, and jumped up like a lunatic.

" 'Ho!' I shouted in a thundering voice, gnashing my teeth, and the fellow became as white as a sheet. He probably thought that I suffered from temporary insanity, but after I had gagged him thoroughly and snatched the revolver he was reaching for, and I had bound his hands and feet securely, I suppose he thought better of me."

"Undoubtedly!" said the listeners.

"But you haven't heard the best of all," continued Blikoortje. "My hands were now free, so I took the corporal's sabre from its sheath and cut through the thick rope with which my feet were bound. I could have gone then, but it was risky in my Boer jacket, and I thought, 'The corporal's coat will fit you too.' "

"Louis escaped in the same way last Saturday," said Karel Wessels.

"So I said to the corporal," Blikoortje continued, " 'I need your coat, my friend, and if ever I can do you a favour someday, just ask for Barend Klaassens.' It was an awkward business, for his hands were tied. I had to undo a few seams fast as lightning and leave behind the sleeves. Anyhow, my mother says 'with sound judgment one can go a long way.' "

"He probably found it very pleasant that you took off his coat?" asked the young Boers, laughing.

"On the contrary. His eyes rolled in his head as if he was a bull gone mad. I was sorry for that, for I was in a good mood, and patting him on the back, I said in a friendly way, 'Don't be cross, mate. You know quite well that I am under pressure!'

"But those friendly words almost led to my downfall, for I had not yet left the tent when an officer entered.

" 'Where is the prisoner?' he called out in a gruff voice.

" 'There!' I said as cool as a cucumber. 'I had to gag him properly, Lieutenant, otherwise he would have woken up all the little children.'

" 'Well done — the garbage!' said the lieutenant, but I dared not set too many demands on his kindness, so I rushed out of the tent, and almost fell over the officer's horse."

"Is that the one you ride now?" asked a Boer.

Blikoortje confirmed this with a nod, and continued his story: "The temptation was too strong for me, boys. I jumped into the saddle. It was a very nice horse — you saw it yourselves: pedigreed, thoroughbred, and in my corporal's coat without sleeves on this beautiful gray horse I felt as happy as a king. I would gladly have hugged the corporal and the lieutenant, such a good laugh did I get from them. I rode to the back of the tent. I was curious how things would end, and in my heart I felt for this unhappy knight of the water wagon.

"At first I heard nothing but a great racket from the officer. Then it became quiet. I suspected that he was removing the gag for this unhappy corporal. I was right, for a moment later I heard his voice. He found it impossible to tell what had happened. He was very agitated, and stammered something terrible.

" 'Well, then sing it,' roared the lieutenant. 'Just sing it, you blockhead!' Then the corporal began singing his recent experience."

The Boers were roaring with laughter.

"There you go, Blikoortje," said the son of a magistrate, "light a cigar — a very nice one from Havana, mind you!"

Blikoortje accepted the cigar with studied elegance, bit off the end, and stuck it between his strong teeth like a born gentleman.

"Well, it was a miserable song," he laughed. "And the lieutenant and I soon had enough of it. He darted out of the tent, maybe in the hope of still speaking to me, but I dug the spurs into the gray. A great commotion arose. The officer made a great hullabaloo, and the Redcoats came running like a swarm of bees that had been disturbed.

" 'There he goes!' cried the officer. 'There!'

" 'Where is he? Where?' shouted the Redcoats.

" 'There — over there!' boomed the lieutenant, but he no longer knew himself, for in the dark and the drizzling rain my gray and I had quickly disappeared from sight."

At this moment the young hunter approached the group.

"Blikoortje," he said, "get up — I must talk to you!"

Chapter XX
Faithful Friends

Louis Wessels had been fortunate enough to track down a Boer commando, and at the unanimous wish of the Afrikaners he was promoted to officer.

He knew that careful reconnoitring was of the utmost importance. Elandslaagte had been a hard lesson and Louis Wessels had no intention of being surprised a second time, as far as he could help it.

Thus he led a hundred Boers into Natal country. They were to do extensive exploration. Besides, Louis was planning to overpower a British convoy.

On their way the company met a Natal labourer who wanted to speak to the leader. Wessels didn't understand what the man had in mind, but dismounted and took the stranger aside.

"Don't you recognize me?" asked the man from Natal.

Louis shook his head.

"You are Mr. Wessels, Mr. Louis Wessels."

The young hunter was astonished.

"Where do you know me from, and who are you?"

"I am Bob," said the man from Natal.

Then Louis did recognize him, but his face clouded over, for his whole being was taken up by the war, and here came this man to elicit a tip from him with some rumour or other.

He felt in his pockets but the man from Natal guessed his thoughts, and said calmly, "I haven't come to beg, Sir. God has blessed me. My wife has recovered, and I earn ample for myself and my family."

Louis felt somewhat ashamed but was likewise surprised.

"I am truly glad for you, Bob!" he said kindly.

"I would like to show you my gratitude by warning you of the treachery lurking in your commandos."

"Treachery?" the young hunter said in disbelief. "You are mistaken, Bob!"

"Your enemy is working with steel and gold," said Bob, "but its gold is more dangerous than its steel."

"Tell me who the traitors are!" Louis said somewhat impatiently.

"I know of one at least," was the answer.

"Well, then name him, Bob!" said Louis on a more friendly note.

"I have forgotten his name, Mr. Wessels."

The young hunter laughed.

"Now you are fooling around, Bobby."

"I'll know the name when I hear it."

The young hunter mentioned some fifteen names, but every time the Natalian shook his head.

"Do you know him, Bob?"

"Yes, I've seen him."

So the Natalian accompanied the young hunter.

The elder Boers sat in small groups smoking, and discussing their chances in the war. The younger ones were throwing clods at one another, and having a marvellous time.

The Natalian shook his head.

"I don't see him here," he said.

The young hunter was becoming irritated. Had this Natalian come here to pull his leg?

He looked at the man with a long, penetrating gaze.

But the Natalian held his own before the hunter's searching look. His callused hands were resting calmly on the long shepherd's staff he had with him. On his broad face, aged prematurely by former suffering, were honesty and good faith.

"Perhaps his name is Blijvenstein?" asked Louis suddenly.

"That's him," answered the Natalian. "Yes, that's it — Blijvenstein!" Satisfaction spread over his broad face.

Once more the young hunter laughed in disbelief.

"Blijvenstein — he is much too afraid for his own skin!"

"Still, it's true, Sir. He is in contact with a black man from these regions who regularly brings over the messages between Blijvenstein and a British officer."

This was a communication of the utmost importance. For a moment Louis was in doubt. No — it was hard to believe such heinous treachery.

"But what is the traitor's intention then?"

"I don't know, Sir. I merely wanted to warn you."

"I thank you Bob," said Wessels cordially. "We must be off now. Will you be seeing Master Arend Uys this week maybe?"

"Tomorrow, I think."

"Give my regards to the family, and tell them that I am still hale and hearty."

So they parted.

The Boers were in their saddles again, and riding hard. They were talking animatedly about intercepting the British convoy. Where the sunken road curved, the young hunter gave the order to halt.

He scaled a high hill, taking his field-glasses.

High up in the sky a swarm of vultures were passing over. They were following the smell of the blood that rose up from the hills of Rietfontein. When the swarm had passed, it was quiet again, but far off a small cloud of dust became visible.

The young hunter fixed all his attention on this cloud. It was becoming bigger — one could now make it out with the naked eye.

"The convoy!" he called in a triumphant voice. He hastened down the hill and gave his orders with the competence of a leader who had grown gray.

The convoy was being dragged along the sandy, sunken road by oxen. For cover there were about forty Natal volunteers swarming like bees around the convoy. They had already discovered the enemy who wanted to surround them. They quickly dismounted, and as they scrambled up the hills which surrounded the sunken road, they opened fire.

"If only I could get the commander!" thought Louis where he lay in perfect safety behind a large rock like a hunter spying on the game. For indeed he was the best marksman in the commando. Even Blikoortje, who was almost sure to hit the bull's-eye at a distance of a hundred paces, could not beat Louis Wessels.

Slowly from behind a stone rose a hat adorned with an ostrich feather that danced in the wind.

"That will be him," thought the young hunter, the frown deepening on his forehead.

"Come out," he muttered. "Just come out!"

Slowly the hat rose, now the eyes were visible, now the face — fire!

But no, the hunter did not fire. For the first time in his life his prey escaped him. He dropped the rifle, and the last drop of blood drained from his face.

He jumped up, waving his hat like a madman to stop the fighting and rushed without weapon toward the enemy.

The Boers were very surprised. They didn't understand, but obeyed him and stopped a battle that had actually not yet begun.

In the meantime Louis Wessels had reached the Natal commander, and shaking his hand, he cried, "John Walker, my friend, my brother! God did not let me shoot you!"

"Louis!" said John. "It's the war, my friend!"

"A true civil war!" groaned Louis.

"How is your father?" asked John kindly.

"Killed!" said Louis.

"And your brothers?"

"Daniel was killed!" said Louis.

"Killed!" repeated the Natal commander.

His eyes became moist and great sorrow filled his soul.

"That you can fight against us!" moaned Louis, and there was great pain in his voice.

"I told you before, Louis, that I would defend this colony if you invaded it. As soon as the commandos retreat from Natal, I'll hang my rifle on the wall."

"We *couldn't* do anything else, John!"

"And I *couldn't* do anything else, Louis. Remember that I was born of English parents and I cannot renounce my own blood. In my opinion you Boers should not have started the war."

"I'll have my men retreat," said Louis. "I intended to attack this convoy, but this time I cannot do it. Go in peace!"

A hesitant look passed over the face of the Natal commander, but it disappeared and, laying his left hand on his friend's shoulder, he pointed with his right toward the horizon.

"I ought not to say this, Louis, but for all the love I received at *Wonderfontein*, I cannot keep quiet — General French is waiting over there with three thousand cavalrymen."

Louis looked at him wide-eyed.

"Within one hour you and your men will be either dead or prisoners unless you turn back immediately."

The Transvaaler's keen eyes brightened.

"So this convoy is intended merely as bait?" he asked.

"Don't ask me any more!" John said slowly. "You people of the Transvaal and the Free State have a lot more to learn! Beware of traitors!"

Louis gave no reply. He took his friend's hand in farewell and pressed it ardently.

Then he gave the order to mount up.

Chapter XXI
The Trail of the Traitor

All this happened during the morning, and Louis owed it to John Walker's faithful friendship that he had escaped the dangerous trap set for him and his hundred Boers.

By now he could hardly doubt that there was a traitor. The confidential communications by Bob and John Walker confirmed each other, and he determined to follow this lead to the best of his ability.

Bob had named Blijvenstein. Well then, Blikoortje was the obvious person to expose the traitor. No one was better qualified than he. And as soon as he had returned to the Boer camp his first task was to look up Blikoortje.

The young hunter found him at a cheerful campfire and called him to one side to give him the startling information.

Blikoortje was not at all surprised. He said he had never trusted the sly, shifty old fellow, and that he had been acting suspiciously that very evening.

Louis Wessels felt as though he was standing on a volcano. It was impossible for him to hide the turmoil which filled his heart with great concern. If he would act on his emotions, he would ask the commander then and there to arrest the innkeeper.

But on which grounds could he do it? He lacked witnesses, and as a free citizen Blijvenstein stood on solid ground. Only when his treason was proved could the criminal be arrested and given the reward he had coming to him. Not before that. And it was of the utmost importance to keep a cool head.

"What do you think, Blikoortje?" said Louis.

The boy fixed his intelligent eyes on the hunter and said in his comical way, "We allow the villain and his English friends to dig a pit, and when it is ready, we throw him into it head over heels."

"Perhaps he is busy digging the pit tonight already."

"The sooner the better!" replied Blikoortje.

Boers on the look-out for the enemy

Suddenly he became excited. His breathing became faster and he said, "Please assign me to keep track of his movements!"

"I was about to ask you to do it," said Louis, "but keep in mind that it might become dangerous!"

Blikoortje was once again as calm as ever.

"Dangerous? It will be more dangerous for him than for me. You can be sure of that."

Again his shrewd eyes looked at the hunter.

"Did he report that a Natal convoy was on the way?"

Louis nodded in confirmation.

"What a character!" Blikoortje burst out. "I thought as much — that he has sold his soul to the god Mammon!"

The two young men parted with a handshake. Blikoortje was not seen again at the campfire that night.

Less than half an hour later Master Blijvenstein left the camp. "My horse has run off," he said to the guard. "It will be quite a job to find the silly animal again."

He had quite some way to walk before reaching the lime tree at the intersection of the transport road, next to some brushwood.

Then he halted and imitated the hoarse cry of a Makau goose, which was answered by a similar cry from the dense leaves of the tree.

Then a human form slid down from the tree.

It was a man in civilian clothes, but the carriage, the tone of voice, the gestures betrayed him as a military man, a British officer.

"I have had to wait very long!" said the Englishman gruffly.

"I couldn't come earlier, Lieutenant."

"I've sat in this confounded tree for an hour and a quarter. The flies were insufferable. They have sucked almost every drop of blood from my body."

"I really couldn't come away earlier, Lieutenant — Wessels seemed very mistrustful tonight."

"We should have taken him today — things went horribly wrong with that convoy."

Master Blijvenstein drew up his shoulders.

"It's not my fault, Lieutenant!"

"Whose fault is it then? Mine, perhaps?"

"I'll explain to you, Lieutenant, what must have happened."

"No please, no explanations from you — you'll have to give an account of yourself before the general."

"I'm a respectable person, Lieutenant, and I don't want to be suspect."

The lieutenant burst out laughing, and lit a cigar.

"You are very funny tonight, Master Blijvenstein. What do you propose now?"

"The commandos of the Boers are moving in a half-circle to the north of Ladysmith, Lieutenant."

"That's old news."

"Really? Who informed you?"

"I myself observed the Boers' position from an air balloon."

Blijvenstein looked cautiously over his shoulder, and said in a muffled voice, "Give me two thousand soldiers, and I will lead them to the right flank of the enemy, to a great position where they can take a whole commando."

"And maybe there won't be an enemy in sight, as it was today with that convoy."

"I'm a respectable man, Lieutenant."

"Yes, of course."

"Didn't my information about the army of Jan Kock turn out to be right? Who could you thank for the victory of Elandslaagte but me? I'm a respectable man, Lieutenant!"

"What you say about Elandslaagte is true. Do you know this vicinity well?"

"I lived here for ten years, and to make quite sure I'll bring along a few black guides. I'll take the soldiers by an absolutely safe route to their destination, and if there is no Boer commando to be nabbed, then . . . what is that rustling in the thornbush?"

"It's nothing, Blijvenstein — go on!"

"If there is no Boer commando to nab, you can hang me, Lieutenant!"

"When did you want to do it?"

"It will have to be at night of course — say, tomorrow night?"

Suddenly he stopped speaking. He had once more heard the suspicious rustling in the bush, and so had the lieutenant.

"Maybe it's a wild cat," he said, throwing a stone in the direction of the bush.

The plaintive moaning of a wild cat ensued.

"There you are!" said the lieutenant reassuringly. "It was only a wild cat."

Then came the financial side of the matter, for Master Blijvenstein definitely the most important part.

The officer offered him twenty pounds for every Boer to be killed or captured in the coming event, and Blijvenstein asked forty pounds. The officer threw in another ten pounds, but Master Blijvenstein was particularly pig-headed, and the lieutenant was glad in the end to haggle an extra five pounds a piece off. In this way the Boers came to be priced at thirty-five pounds each.

Blijvenstein received fifty gold sovereigns as an earnest on the spot, and after agreeing on a few more essential matters, they each went their way.

The thornbush began to rustle again. A shadow appeared. It followed Master Blijvenstein.

When he slowed down to feel the fifty gold pieces he had in his pocket, the shadow also slowed down. When he thought of the suspicion that might arise from his absence, and started walking faster, the shadow also accelerated.

He had now come near the guard.

"Don't shoot, Cousin!" he said, passing quickly.

"Haven't you found your horse?" asked the guard.

"No, Cousin, not yet — it's a great bother!" said Master Blijvenstein, walking toward the campfires.

Restless to an extent he had never known before, Louis Wessels sat waiting for Blikoortje. The wait was not in vain, however, for the boy brought with him very serious news.

"So, he is a traitor, Blikoortje?"

"A grandson to Beelzebub himself!" answered the boy. And he made a complete report. His tone was graver than usual, and when he told how Master Blijvenstein had the bloody defeat at Elandslaagte on his conscience, Louis snatched up his rifle. The next moment he had regained his self-control. He returned the rifle to its corner of the tent, and said calmly, "Carry on. I'm listening with great interest."

Chapter XXII
The Young Hunter

The night was dark.

On a rocky ridge stood the young hunter, all by himself. His hands were resting on the shiny barrel of his Mauser.

There was no campfire near him, even his pipe had been put away. There was not a spark to betray him.

Stretched out at his feet lay his dog.

He stood motionless against the trunk of a huge oak. It seemed as though he was one with the trunk.

It was quiet, but a night bird approached with slow wing-beat and landed in the top of the oak, above the hunter.

The dog growled softly.

"Quiet, Pluto," said the hunter. "Quiet!"

The dog was silent again.

The night wind went wailing through the dry spiky grass on the rocky hill, and from afar came the sound of approaching hooves. But the sound receded and died down again.

Listen, what was that?

It was the roar of a hungry wild animal.

Pluto jumped up. But his young master patted him lightly on the head and he lay down again.

Then a loud sharp cry was heard. The dog gave tongue, loudly and furiously.

"Quiet, Pluto!" said the hunter. "It's only the nightbird up there!"

The bird of prey opened its heavy wings, breaking the twigs, and disappeared in the dark.

Young Wessels stood quietly, without making the slightest movement. He was truly a born hunter, for he had patience, perseverance, and strength. He had stood in that place for two hours already, and if necessary, he would patiently stand there for twelve times two hours.

But now a peculiar tremor ran through his limbs. His tall figure seemed to grow still taller. His nostrils quivered; a sudden light passed through his eyes.

The hunter had smelled the game.

The dog pricked its ears and jumped up.

"Quiet, Pluto!" said its master softly but with emphasis. "Lie down!"

The dog lay down again, moving its tail slightly and sniffing the air.

Then came the sound of creaking wagons and clattering wheels. Slowly but surely the sound came nearer. Now the sound of stamping hooves and the lowing of oxen could be heard.

Hundreds of soldiers were approaching. Their footsteps could be heard.

"What is this?" came a subdued voice.

"A sunken road," answered a second voice.

"This is an Egyptian darkness," said the first.

"But the whiskey makes it lighter," said the second, taking a sizeable swig from his field flask.

Then came the mules. The young hunter heard the grating of the light mountain cannon lashed to the animals' backs with strong leather straps.

His foot knocked one of a number of large loose stones on the ground, and suddenly a plan took form in his mind.

He leaned his rifle against the trunk of the oak, and rolled a few of the stones right up to the edge where the rocky hill dropped almost vertically. Then he lay down flat on the ground and tried to peer into the darkness below him. But even his hawk-eyes could not make out much more than vague outlines. His ears, however, were wide open, and he laid his muscular hands on the first stone. But he drew back again — the right moment had not yet come.

It was a small cavalry division passing below.

Then — with a powerful thrust he sent the first stone over the edge. It fell into a scraggy thornbush making a meagre existence in the steep hillside, breaking its branches, and struck the ground in front of the hooves of one of the horses.

The driver grabbed the skittish animal just in time and tightened the reins. But then there was a second rock — a third — a fourth.

The fifth fell in the middle of an ammunition wagon, and the mules harnessed to it made a dash for it. The drivers were swearing and jumping in front of the horses to stop them, but their foolish shouting made the animals even more skittish. They collided with other mule teams, and so increased the fright and confusion.

The officers were making superhuman efforts to save the cannon and the ammunition wagons, but the rocks kept coming down. The frenzied mules fled to the left, trampling the officers underfoot.

"Grab the mules!" cried the officers, but the drivers and the soldiers were ill at ease themselves, and stared upward to the dark ridge from which invisible hands were hurling heavy rocks to the ground below.

The young hunter lay peering over the edge of the ridge with a taut face, but as the confusion down below came to a climax and the braying mules, maddened by the rumbling of the wagons behind them, dashed off in unstoppable panic, followed by the futile cries of excited soldiers, a huge smile spread over his face.

It was the first smile since Elandslaagte.

He jumped up from the hard ground and descended the other side of the rocky ridge, whistling for his horse. Less than twenty seconds later he was in the saddle. The bay struck out its iron-shod hooves so that sparks flew from the stones with which the *veld* was strewn. He only slowed his gallop when the secret signal lights showed that there were Boer guards near.

Chapter XXIII
The Traitor's End

The young hunter looked back for a moment.

He counted his men — one hundred and twenty resolute young men.

"This is the way the two battalions went," he said. "Forward!"

It was a fine sight. The horses' heads touched one another; the rifle barrels shone in the morning light as the horsemen sped past swiftly, like the whirlwinds which howl over the African plains.

From afar could clearly be heard the sound of gunfire. They had reached the battlefield. Louis Wessels gave the order to halt.

Before them stretched the hill called Nicholsnek. It was occupied by two battalions of British infantry, to whom the traitor Blijvenstein had acted as guide, and who — to their utmost surprise — had already been received by lively Free State gunfire from various hills.

Quickly Louis ordered the horses to be unsaddled and brought to safety, and his men to take up their positions.

But now he felt the full weight of his responsibility as leader and the seriousness of the situation.

"Comrades!" he said. "Brothers! Let us pray!"

He knelt down. Everyone followed his example, deeply stirred.

And Louis Wessels prayed: "Almighty God, God of our fathers! We trust in Thee, only in Thee. Thou hast been our Refuge from generation to generation. Teach our hands how to fight. Gird us, and we will do great deeds! We do not call on dumb idols, but on Thee, the living God. Have mercy on our souls and on the souls of our enemies, and grant us the victory on this day, in the Name of Jesus. Amen!"

The Boers got up from their knees. The young hunter stretched out his hand and pointed to the top of Nicholsnek.

"The summit is our aim," he said calmly. "Take it!"

Cautiously but with determination Wessels's men advanced, and slowly gained ground. They did not expose themselves unnecessarily, but they were all excellent marksmen, and the English who looked out were shot down like rock pigeons.

Louis looked sideways for a moment. His two brothers lay, sheltered by rocks, in a line with him. A fighting spirit sparked from their eyes.

Then the young hunter took a huge leap forward to reach another rock, but Karel did a real leopard jump and landed next to him, behind the same rock.

"What's that!" asked Louis anxiously when he saw blood on Karel's hands.

"Nothing, dear brother!" said Karel. "Just a scratch on the skin!" and he laughed heartily.

Kees approached, very excited.

"I've seen him!" he said.

"Who?" asked Louis, and his heart beat faster.

"The traitor!"

"Blijvenstein?"

Kees nodded affirmation. He was pale with emotion and pointed in the direction where he thought he had seen the traitor.

The young hunter peered from behind the rocks but his hawk-eyes could not discover the traitor.

"I don't see him," he said.

"He's hiding behind that thick tree-trunk over there. Come, Louis, you go to the left, and I'll go to the right. You shoot at the tree, and to get better cover the traitor will have to let himself be seen for a moment — and I'll take him out!"

But Louis shook his head.

"*You* must flush him out," he said, "and *I'll* pick him off."

"Why?" was Kees's surprised question. "Don't you trust my shooting? Didn't I just hit that officer at four hundred metres?"

"My hand will take him out, Kees."

"He has the battle of Elandslaagte on his conscience, and so also the death of our father and brother — allow me to do it, Louis, I beg you!" His voice was hoarse with emotion.

But Louis laid a hand on his shoulder. The Wessels traits were sharply evident in both their faces.

134

"No, Brother," he said in a friendly but firm voice. "The task is mine as the eldest son. But then, without you I cannot do it either. So go, and flush out the traitor!"

So Kees went, and both took up new positions: Kees to the left and Louis to the right.

In silence the young hunter lay behind the hard rock, his hawk-eyes fixed on the tree. His face seemed etched in stone. The gun barrel lay motionless in his left hand. Slowly, almost imperceptibly, the finger of his right hand went to the trigger.

"Come now, Kees," he spoke to himself. "Chase him out!"

All of a sudden, there it was! A dark, threatening frown between the eyebrows — a flash of light in the blue eyes — a shaft of fire from the rifle!

And two paces from the tree which Blijvenstein had left to seek better cover, the young hunter's bullet picked off the traitor!

The Boers were advancing slowly. A ring of steel and fire began closing around Nicholsnek and the terrified soldiers began suspecting that they had walked into an awful trap.

Now and then an Englishman would look over the barricade, just to see the African scenery and the African sun for the last time. The British officers stared at the horizon, in the hope that General White would send help, but from afar came the cheering of the Boers who had already defeated the enemy in other parts of the battlefield. For this battle, which the Boers called the Battle of Modderspruit, stretched over several miles and was the biggest battle that had thus far been fought between two white races in South Africa.

Of the fourteen hundred soldiers on Nicholsnek more than two hundred lay dead or wounded on the hill.

Only on one side was there still a gap where one could escape, but this was quickly filled by Boers coming up from below — ten, twenty, sixty men — with one strong man leaping ahead.

His cheeks were glowing and his eyes shone.

"For freedom and justice!" he called out in a ringing voice. "Forward!"

Yes, it was the hunter, the great hunter, and who could stand against him?

The officers commanded, "Fire!" but the soldiers cast away their arms, and tried to flee. They were now closed in on all sides, and they could see that they had been captured like game in a net.

"Drop your weapons!" called the young hunter, and they went down.

"Hands up!" he called again, and they went up.

An officer was sitting on a rock. He was exhausted from the long fight, and his usually severe face was sorrowful.

"Your sword!" said Louis.

The officer rose, and stared into the Boer's face for a moment, then handed over the sword without a word, while tears sprang to the brave man's eyes.

Then Louis recognized the small major from Elandslaagte, and gave the beaten man a friendly hand.

"Keep your sword!" he said.

And when the major looked at him questioningly, he resumed, "You gave me my freedom at Elandslaagte — now I give you your freedom. That's what I mean, Major!"

In silence they stood together for a moment.

"I'll write you a letter of safe-conduct in a moment," said Louis. "What else can I do for you?"

The major complained of thirst. Louis gave him his field flask, and he quenched his thirst.

Louis tore a page from his notebook, wrote a few words on it, and handed the officer the safe conduct.

The Englishman was deeply moved. He put his hands on Wessels's shoulders, and said in an emotional voice, "Isn't it terrible that we should stand against one another as enemies? Will we never be granted the luxury to join ranks against a common enemy? Will the fires of contention always burn between the Boers and the British?"

"God knows!" said Louis. He sighed.

And so they parted.

The battle had ended. The prisoners of war were taken away. Accompanied by both of his brothers and Blikoortje, the young hunter was striding over the battlefield. His eye was fixed on the big tree behind which Blijvenstein had sought cover, and he found

The British defeated at Modderspruit

the traitor. His features were distorted, his hand on the right side of his chest.

"That's where his money is!" said Blikoortje, pointing to the hand.

A few men came past with stretchers. They were collecting the dead and taking them away to the huge grave that was being dug.

But the young hunter shook his head.

"Let him lie!" he said, in a voice now stern and hard, "as a deterrent for all traitors!"

So the traitor was left to lie there.

Chapter XXIV
Beside a Grave

In the afternoon of that memorable day, after the British soldiers had been driven back into Ladysmith by the triumphant Boer commandos, three people presented themselves to one of the Boer commanders. All three were in mourning garments.

"What is it you want to know?" asked the bearded commander kindly.

"My daughter and I," said the eldest, a middle-aged woman, "have come by train from the Transvaal, for we received the terrible news that my husband and our youngest son were killed at Elandslaagte. I have three more sons in this horrible war, and you will understand that a mother's heart can't find any rest."

"Are you the widow of Gijs Wessels?" asked the commander with sincere sympathy.

"I am," she replied.

"Your husband died for his people."

"He did," she answered.

"So Louis Wessels is also your son?" he now asked.

"Yes," she said, and it looked as if she was stabbed in the heart.

"Don't worry," he comforted her. "Louis Wessels is the hero of the day — the Lion of Modderspruit!"

"And my two other sons?" she asked with maternal anxiety.

"They are alive and well — I'll find them for you."

He called an aide, and gave him the orders required.

He was a fast one, the aide.

In forty minutes' time he was back, and not alone either.

The three young Boers who accompanied him leaped from their saddles and embraced their mother.

What a poignant reunion!

The commander turned his back, wiping away a few tears with a rough hand.

"We heard the roaring of the cannon today," said Mother Wessels, "and we called on God, all three of us, for your precious lives!"

Late in the evening of this day the family group could once more be seen, not on the battlefield of Modderspruit, but on the battlefield of Elandslaagte.

The terrain still bore many marks of the devastating battle. Near a broken ox wagon whose canvas had been shot to shreds by cannon-balls, and a spiked cannon lying on its side, lay the stony hill under which Gijs Wessels and his son Daniel were sleeping the long sleep of the dead.

Near the grave, in a quiet and peaceful place, they sat down.

The young hunter sat next to his mother. Opposite him sat Truida and Janske. Truida was wearing the sober dress of a Sister of Mercy of the Red Cross. Louis was holding his mother's hands between his own strong hands. Kees and Karel sat kneeling beside her.

The heavy and deeply painful loss they had been dealt had brought the surviving family members all the more close together. So it is with a shared grief. It binds more strongly than joy.

Now Louis was telling what had befallen him. Truida, too, was mentioned in it. How could it be otherwise?

Mother Wessels's hand went slowly and caressingly over Truida's head.

"I never had misgivings about you, my little daughter," she said tenderly. "I knew very well that in his own time the Lord would tear the blindfold from your eyes and let you see on which side justice and truth lie."

In this answer emerged once more the true Afrikaans woman whose heart felt for justice, freedom, and for the fatherland.

Kees also told of what had befallen him — the murderous battle at Talana Hill, where he had stood for eight hours under a rain of bombs that made the Natal hills tremble.

The moon had now risen above the shining horizon and a deep and wonderful peace descended on the landscape. Nothing was heard on this quiet summer evening but the quiet voices of these people who loved one another so deeply.

"But you haven't told me anything," said Mother Wessels to Karel, who was now her youngest son.

He pressed closer to his mother and said, "In the Battle of Talana Hill one of our burghers saw a seriously-wounded English cavalry man lying in the *veld*. As the burgher passed the wounded man, the trooper asked for water; he was dying of thirst. So the burgher, whose name was Botha, held out a flask to him. But the man was too weak to take the flask, and Botha got down from his horse, lifted the dying man's head, and refreshed him. He looked at the burgher with gratitude in his eyes, and enquired about the two leaders who were riding up and down to the right and the left of the Transvaal army, encouraging and inciting the fighting soldiers. They wore white clothes and sat on white horses, each holding a flag.

" 'I don't know that flag,' continued the dying man. 'How we fired on them, but all in vain. Our best marksmen could not hit them.'

"Our burgher shook his head, for he did not know the generals, and the dying man said, 'They must have been angels.' And then he died . . ."

A light wind sprang up. The blades of grass were rustling. The treetops moved as if in a dream.

It was late.

Christiaan was approaching with the Basotho pony, meant for Truida. And the following day Mother Wessels and Janske were to leave for *Wonderfontein* again.

Mother Wessels got up. The moon shone on her face full of character, made nobler by grief; but her eyes shone with a light that showed she was recovering.

Her strong young sons stood before her.

"My children," she said, "my dear children! Now we must leave you, but God will not leave you. Your father and your brother died as heroes for a just cause. They did not fight for themselves, but to retain the holy gift that Almighty God has entrusted to our people. And they will shine like stars for ever and ever, because they have been true unto death!"

For a moment she was quiet.

Her eyes were gazing far into the night like the eyes of a prophetess.

But Louis could contain himself no longer.

"Mother, oh, Mother!" He burst into sobs. "Now you will be just a poor, weak widow!"

"Do not cry for me, my son," said she, "for I do not cry for you. Your father rests here under the hard stones — now Almighty God will be your Father. I am a widow, but He will be my Judge, my Judge against England!"

"Do not cry for me, children," she resumed with tenderness, "but cry for the poor, poor queen of England whose gray hair, when she rests in her coffin soon, will be spattered with the innocent blood of two small nations!"

"Will we gain the victory?" asked Karel softly.

"Yes, my son," she said in a firm voice, "our people will gain the victory."

"Will it be soon, Mother?" he asked.

"My child," she said in a reprimanding tone and airing the thoughts of her fallen husband, "how can you ask that! The struggle of the Afrikaans people against the mighty England began with the murder at Slachtersnek — this war is just a new and harder and more bloody stage in this long struggle. Our people have now struggled for eighty-five years, and we do not know when the struggle will end. Perhaps with this war — perhaps in fifty years' time — who can tell? Yes, our people may be overcome temporarily, and yet the struggle will end with a victory! The great Smelter has started refining the gold. And when the gold has been refined in the oven, He will put out the fire!"

She laid her hands on the heads of her sons. They knelt before her.

"My prayers, dear children," she said slowly, tears audible in her voice, "will go up for you day and night. May the God of your fathers bless you, and fill your hearts with strength and the courage of heroes!"

The three rose again.

Mother Wessels embraced them and kissed them. Then they took leave of Janske and Truida.

"God be with you, Louis!" Truida added.

"And God bless you in your work of charity!" said Louis from his heart.

Then they parted.

And Gijs Wessels and his son Daniel remained behind alone on the field of the dead in Elandslaagte.

There they sleep, under the hard rocks of Natal. Perhaps they will have to sleep for a long time before awaking. But they will awake — and a happy awakening it will be!

For the night will pass, and with it the darkness and the violence done by the unjust; and the morning will come, the joyful morning for which our prayerful hearts wait!

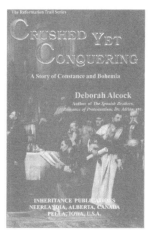

Crushed Yet Conquering
by Deborah Alcock

A gripping story filled with accurate historical facts about John Huss and the Hussite wars. **Hardly any historical novel can be more captivating and edifying than this book.** Even if Deborah Alcock was not the greatest of nineteenth century authors, certainly she is our most favourite.

— Roelof & Theresa Janssen

Time: 1414-1436   **Age: 11-99**
ISBN 1-894666-01-1   **Can.$19.95 U.S.$14.90**

The Spanish Brothers by Deborah Alcock

Christine Farenhorst in *Christian Renewal*: This historical novel, which is set in Spain a number of years after the Reformation, deals with the discovery of Reformed truth in that country . . . Two brothers, one a soldier and the other a student of theology, are the protagonists. Sons of a nobleman who disappeared when they were children, their search for him leads both to a confrontation with the Gospel. How they react, how their friends and relatives react to them, and what their struggles and thoughts are, form the main body of the book.

An excellent read, this book should be in every church and home library.

Time: 1550-1565   **Age: 14-99**
ISBN1-894666-02-x   **Can.$14.95 U.S.$12.90**

By Far Euphrates by Deborah Alcock
A Tale on Armenia in the 19th century

Alcock has provided sufficient graphics describing the atrocities committed against the Armenian Christians to make the reader emotionally moved by the intense suffering these Christians endured at the hands of Muslim Turks and Kurds. At the same time, the author herself has confessed to not wanting to provide full detail, which would take away from the focus on how those facing death did so with peace, being confident they would go to see their LORD, and so enjoy eternal peace. **As such it is not only an enjoyable novel, but also encouraging reading.** These Christians were determined to remain faithful to their God, regardless of the consequences.

Time: 1887-1895   **Age: 11**
ISBN 1-894666-00-3   **Can.$14.95 U.S.$12**

Coronation of Glory
by Deborah Meroff

The true story of seventeen-year-old Lady Jane Grey, Queen of England for nine days.

"Miss Meroff . . . has fictionalized the story of Lady Jane Grey in a thoroughly absorbing manner . . . she has succeeded in making me believe this is what really happened. I kept wanting to read on — the book is full of action and interest."
— Elisabeth Elliot

Time: 1537-1554   **Age: 14-99**
ISBN 0-921100-78-7   **Can.$14.95 U.S.$12.90**

Captain My Captain by Deborah Meroff

Willy-Jane VanDyken in *The Trumpet*: This romantic novel is so filled with excitement and drama, it is difficult to put it down once one has begun it. Its pages reflect the struggle between choosing Satan's ways or God's ways. Mary's struggles with materialism, being a submissive wife, coping with the criticism of others, learning how to deal with sickness and death of loved ones, trusting in God and overcoming the fear of death forces the reader to reflect on his own struggles in life. This story of Mary Ann Patten (remembered for being the first woman to take full command of a merchant sailing ship) is one that any teen or adult reader will enjoy. It will perhaps cause you to shed a few tears but it is bound to touch your heart and encourage you in your faith.

Time: 1837-1861   **Age: 14-99**
ISBN 0-921100-79-5   **Can.$14.95 U.S.$12.90**

Journey Through the Night
by Anne De Vries

After the second world war, Anne De Vries, one of he most popular novelists in The Netherlands, was mmissioned to capture in literary form the spirit agony of those five harrowing years of Nazi ation. The result was Journey Through the a four volume bestseller that has gone more than thirty printings in The Nether-

stament Professor of mine who bought ld not put them down — nor could I."
— Dr. Edwin H. Palmer

99
90

-6   **Age: 10-99**
        Can.$19.95 U.S.$14.90

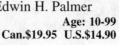